JENNINGS' DIARY

Jennings is suffering from beginning-of-term-itis, but things soon return to the normal state of mayhem when his new diary is made public property! Alarmed at the thought of his most private thoughts being made public, Jennings invents a secret language. Inspired by a visit to the Natural History Museum, Jennings and Darbishire establish their own collection of ancient relics, but they are not out of trouble for long and when the precious diary goes missing, Jennings finds himself on the wrong side of the law!

JENNINGS' DIARY

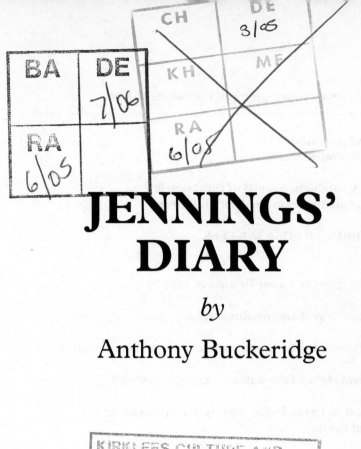
JENNINGS' DIARY

by

Anthony Buckeridge

Dales Large Print Books
Long Preston, North Yorkshire,
BD23 4ND, England.

British Library Cataloguing in Publication Data.

Buckeridge, Anthony
    Jennings' diary.

    A catalogue record of this book is
    available from the British Library

    ISBN   1-84262-367-2 pbk

First published in Great Britain in 1955

Dales Large Print is an imprint of Library Magna Books Ltd.

Printed and bound in Great Britain by
T.J. (International) Ltd., Cornwall, PL28 8RW

For Martin

The Jennings books of Anthony Buckeridge span the years 1950–2000. Many social changes occurred during this time including the adoption of decimal currency in 1971 to replace that of pounds, shillings and pence. This edition contains all the original writings of Anthony Buckeridge and has not been altered or changed in any way.

Contents

1 The Start of It All   15
2 Top Secret   31
3 Jennings Finds an Ally   41
4 The Scarlet Runner   53
5 So Long at the Fair   67
6 The Present for Matron   79
7 Assorted Fossils   95
8 The Rattling Relic   111
9 The Root of the Trouble   127
10 Wrong Side of the Law   141
11 The Genuine Fake   161
12 On View to the Public   173
13 Mr Wilkins Rides Alone   189
14 Knotty Problem   207
15 Jennings Tries his Hand   225
16 Pack Up Your Troubles!   241

1

The Start of It All

The first evening of a new term is just a little different from all the other evenings which lie ahead. It is a restless, unsettled time when ties with home have been broken, and the links of another term are not yet forged.

Jennings sat on his bed, twirling his socks round and round like contra-rotating propellers and puzzling over this feeling of strangeness which was taking so long to wear off. He knew it was nothing to do with his surroundings, for Linbury Court Preparatory School looked the same as it always had done. The dormitory seemed familiar enough, with its rows of beds and lockers and chairs; there was the well-remembered damp patch on the ceiling caused by the overflowing of a washbasin in the room above; below this, the mark on the wall where a badly aimed sponge bag had overshot the target area. All these were unchanged. What, then, was wrong?

Perhaps it was his friends who were different! After all, it was a whole month since he had seen them. He gazed about him, seeking a clue to the mystery.

All round the dormitory, boys were preparing for bed – struggling with knotted shoe laces, or straining pullovers into shapeless woollen tunnels as they tugged them over their heads. Yet no one appeared to have changed very much, Jennings thought; apart, of course, from the minor alterations which were only to be expected on the first day of term.

Venables, for instance, was still suffering from a recent drastic haircut which caused him to massage the bristly nape of his neck every few seconds. And Darbishire was wearing a new suit, specially chosen to allow him plenty of room to grow in all directions. No doubt the time would come when it would fit him well enough, but at the moment his slight figure appeared to be shrouded in a loosely woven cocoon of grey tweed. The sleeves, reaching almost to his knuckles, had caused him trouble all through teatime, by sliding down on to his plate and becoming mixed up with his bread and butter.

Jennings stopped twirling his socks and called: 'I say, Darbishire, are you feeling all right?'

It was the first time he had spoken to his friend since they had parted company at the end of the previous term; but theirs was an easy-going friendship which bridged the gap of absence without effort, and started off again quite naturally from where it had left off.

'Yes, I think so,' Darbishire replied, slipping off his jacket. 'At any rate, I'm feeling a lot better now I've found my way out of this suit. Why, don't I *look* all right?'

'Oh yes; I just wondered whether you were feeling like me. Sort of – queer, if you know what I mean.'

'It must have been those baked beans we had for tea,' said Darbishire. 'You want to be careful with baked beans; they need watching. I found one up my sleeve when I took my jacket off just now.' He stared earnestly at his friend through dusty spectacles. 'You lie down quietly, if you're feeling rotten. I'll go and fetch Matron; she'll soon put you right.'

Jennings clicked his teeth in mild exasperation. 'Don't be such a clodpoll, Darbi! I'm not ill.'

'You said you were.'

'No, I didn't. I meant there was a peculiar sort of *something* in the air. I wondered whether you'd noticed it.'

Darbishire removed his glasses and peered round the room. The atmosphere looked all right to him. 'We could open the window if you like,' he suggested helpfully.

'It's not that. It's a sort of feeling I've got: rather as though I've been here before.'

17

'Well, so you have; every night for the last four terms. If you want to know what *I* think, Jennings, I'd say you were suffering from a pretty chronic attack of beginning-of-term-itis.'

'Uh?'

'Oh, it's nothing serious. It's just that you haven't switched over properly from holidays to term time.' The specialist frowned thoughtfully at his patient. 'You'll feel less chronic tomorrow when you've got over the ghastly shock, and after that you'll settle down to a calm and peaceful term with everything running smoothly.'

A rash prophecy if ever there was one! Jennings' feeling of strangeness passed quickly enough, but it is doubtful whether 'calm and peaceful' was a fair description of the storm-tossed breakers ahead in the troubled waters of the Easter term.

Pleased with this ready solution of his friend's problem, Darbishire returned to his bed, rolled up his new suit into a tight ball, and screwed it into his clothes locker.

Jennings, meanwhile, was unpacking the small suitcase which contained the things he would need for the first night of term. He laid his pyjamas on his bed and placed his still damp flannel and soap neatly on the top, while he rummaged through the remaining contents of his case. At once a look of concern clouded his wide-awake eyes; his

18

collection of cheese labels was there safely enough; so were his match-box tops and propelling pencil; but where was his diary? Surely he hadn't left it at home!

Worried now, he tipped the case upside down over his bed and searched through the collection of bedroom slippers, hair brushes, and the stack of a dozen handkerchiefs which his mother had felt sure he would need before his trunk was unpacked the following day.

Still no diary!... This was serious; for it had been a Christmas present from his Aunt Angela, and so far he had kept his New Year's resolution of recording an entry every day. Perhaps it was in his jacket pocket?... No, it wasn't there either. Then where on earth...?

A loud crow of gleeful triumph came from beyond the washbasins at the other end of the room.

'Wacko, I've found something!' And there was Venables waving a small red book round his head like a tomahawk.

'Hey Venables; that's my diary!' Jennings called down the room. 'I've been looking for it everywhere. Where did you find it?'

'Where did you lose it?' countered Venables, a tall, thin boy of twelve. 'You'll have to prove it's yours if you want it back. Otherwise, it's "findings, keepings".'

'It must have dropped out of my pocket.

It's mine all right. My Aunt Angela gave it to me. Be decent and give it back.' Jennings advanced to the washbasins with hand out-stretched. He seemed so anxious for the safe return of his property that Venables noticed his concern and determined to make the most of his advantage.

'It doesn't say anything about anybody's Aunt Angela here,' he said, thumbing through the pages. 'How do I know it's really yours? I shall have to hang on to it while I investigate the matter.'

'Of *course* it's mine, you ancient ruin,' persisted Jennings. 'It's got my name inside. You can read, can't you?'

Venables paused at a page marked *Personal Memoranda*. 'It says here,' he began, 'that this diary belongs to a character called J C T Jennings; age last birthday – 11; size in boots – 4; size in collars – 13; insurance policy number – blank; business address...'

Jennings made a grab at the book, but Venables whisked it out of reach and held it over a washbasin full of water. 'Don't snatch,' he said. 'I might drop it in by accident if you do, and then it won't be worth having back, anyway. I haven't finished my investigations yet.' He turned a page and read aloud:

'January 1st: Got up... Had breakfast... Did some things... Weather quite hot toddy...'

'January 2nd: Got up... Went out... Came

back... Did some more things... Weather not so hot toddy.'

'Hey you can't read that; it's private!' Jennings protested.

Venables grinned. 'Sounds as though you had a pretty exciting holiday. Fancy going out *and* coming back all in one day! I don't quite follow this "hot toddy" business, though. Is it something to drink?'

'No, you bazooka. You can't read straight. It's not "hot toddy" – it's *hot today*. Aunt Angela told me to make notes about the weather. She's going to give me ten shillings if I write something every day and never miss once.'

Again Venables glanced at the book in his hand, and then hooted in derisive glee. 'I say gather round, you chaps... Special news bulletin from Jennings' famous diary!'

Temple, Atkinson and Bromwich major postponed their knee-washing operations until a more convenient time, and came crowding round to see what all the excitement was about.

'Don't be a rotter, Venables! Give it back,' Jennings protested. 'You've no right to *look* at a chap's private diary let alone broadcast it all over the school.' He thrust out his hand to grab the book – and then withdrew it again quickly as Venables made a further move towards the washbasins.

'Listen to this, you chaps.' Venables

quoted: *'January 5th: Listened for cuckoo, but did not hear it.'*

The audience rocked with mirth, and tapped their foreheads pityingly at the diarist's quaint zoological observations.

'He should have listened to himself;' said Temple. 'He's as cuckoo as a coot, if you ask me.'

'Well, I *did* listen,' Jennings defended himself. 'I knew I shouldn't hear it, but Aunt Angela's ever so keen on nature and stuff, and I was trying to please her.'

But no one was listening to his explanation, for already Venables was reading the extract for *January 7th.* The announcement: *Went to Nat. Hist. Mus.* was received with puzzled expressions.

'Went *where?*' queried Atkinson.

'*Nat. Hist. Mus.*,' replied Venables. 'That's what it says here, anyway. Perhaps it's in code.'

'Of course it isn't,' said Jennings. 'It means Natural History Museum. Aunt Angela took me there after Christmas; I told you she was keen on nature and things, even when they're stuffed.'

'Went to Nat. Hist. Mus. – soon after Christmus,' recited Bromwich major. 'I say you chaps, did you hear that? I've just made up a poem, by accident. I said...'

'All right, we heard; and a pretty feeble effort, too.' Venables turned to the poet with a snort of disapproval, and so failed to notice Jennings stealthily removing the plug from the washbasin.

As the last drops of water trickled out, Jennings hurled himself upon Venables in a neck-high rugger tackle. Venables dropped the diary into the basin and discovered, too late, that his threatened reprisal had lost its effect. Jennings grabbed the book as it slithered down the damp side of the washbasin: the next second he had backed away, dodged round the group of interested spectators and was skidding full-tilt along the linoleum which ran the length of the room.

'After him, quick!' cried Venables, delighted at this extension of the game. 'Tackle him low. He's a foreign spy escaping with the secret plans!'

Atkinson and Temple joined the chase, their toothbrushes pointed revolver-fashion at the fugitive, while the sharp crack of imaginary shots clicked and rattled from the back of their throats.

Jennings was enjoying himself as much as his pursuers, for it was a friendly feud with no ill-will behind it. All the same, the rules demanded that the game must be played as though their lives depended upon the outcome. There must be no crying of 'pax' unless a master was sighted, no retiring from this slaughter of a thousand deaths unless some luckless opponent accidentally bumped his head or barked his shins, as a result of not looking where he was going.

At the door, Jennings turned, clicked out a volley of machine-gun fire and then sped flat-out along the corridor. He must hide!... Somewhere... Anywhere! The diary's safety was no longer important: it had now become the excuse for a lively bout of spy-chasing before the duty master appeared to turn out the dormitory lights.

He turned the corner and shot in through the open doorway of Dormitory 3. Eight boys, in various stages of getting ready for bed, eyed him with interest.

'What's the rush?' asked Thompson minor, pausing in the act of climbing between the sheets.

'I'm being attacked. I want somewhere to hide,' gasped Jennings. But Dormitory 3 offered little cover for a foreign spy escaping from counter-espionage agents: a locked clothes cupboard, and a row of beds and chairs accounted for most of the furniture.

A bed near the door was empty, its occupant out of the room on some mysterious errand. Jennings wasted no time. He dived into the bed and pulled the sheets up about his ears, so that only a tangle of brown hair was visible. His closed eyes and heavy breathing gave the impression of profound sleep, though in point of fact sleep of any sort would have been out of the question amid the noisy preparations for bed that were going on around the room.

The ruse was good enough to deceive Venables, when his close-cropped head peered round the door a moment later.

'Any of you characters seen a mysterious foreign agent around these parts?' he inquired hopefully

'No,' chorused Dormitory 3, smirking with glee at this chance to throw the pursuers off the scent with a truthful answer.

Venables glanced along the row of beds; his eye passed without suspicion over the mound beneath the bedclothes. 'That's funny; I thought he came in here.'

'Maybe he went this way,' suggested Binns minor, pointing left.

'Perhaps he went that way,' volunteered Martin-Jones, jerking his thumb in the opposite direction.

'Well, it doesn't matter much. He'll turn up before lights out.' Disappointed, Venables led the trigger-happy pursuit party away, just as the owner of the borrowed bed arrived back from the bathroom.

It had taken the rightful tenant some time to find the way to his dormitory. He was a new boy named Blotwell; and for the last ten minutes he had been wandering about, hopelessly lost in the maze of corridors which all looked alike on his first evening in the building.

Then, passing the open door of Dormitory 3, he had recognised a clothes cupboard that he thought he had seen before. With renewed hope he turned into the room. Yes, this was the place; he was sure of it now... Or was he?

For the bed which he hoped might be his was already occupied. Furthermore, the occupier appeared so deeply asleep, and was snoring so loudly that he seemed unlikely to awaken before morning.

Blotwell sighed... Wrong again! He had had no idea that boarding school would turn out to be such a confusing sort of place. Glumly he trailed out of the dormitory, and set off once more along the endless corridors in his quest for somewhere to spend the night.

The master on duty in the dormitories that evening was Mr Wilkins, a large bustling man with a powerful voice which made his lightest whisper sound as thought it was being amplified through a megaphone. His tone was brisk and his temper a little uncertain; for though he liked boys well enough, he was constantly baffled by the things they chose to do, and the bewildering way in which their minds appeared to work.

He was, therefore, a little puzzled, when going round the dormitories, to find a small, dressing-gowned figure camping out on the landing, with a bath towel spread over him in the form of a counterpane.

'What on earth are you doing there?' demanded Mr Wilkins.

'I couldn't find a bed to sleep in, sir. Everywhere was booked up when I looked.'

'I think you've made a mistake about that,' said Mr Wilkins, switching on his kindliest tone to put the new boy at his ease. 'Let me see, you're – er ... Blotwell, aren't you?'

The camper admitted his identity.

'Well, you come with me, Blotwell, and we'll soon put you right. You're probably in Dormitory 3.' And the master strode off with the small figure trailing hopefully at his heels.

Jennings was just about to leave his hiding place when he heard Mr Wilkins' heavy footfall on the landing outside. He had delayed going back to his own room until Venables and his spy hunters should have had time to find some other form of amusement. And now it seemed he had delayed too long, for the rules of Linbury Court School were quite definite on the subject of boys who entered a dormitory to which they did not belong.

Escape was clearly out of the question, so Jennings continued to feign sleep with the sheet pulled well over his ears.

'Here we are, Blotwell,' boomed Mr

Wilkins, striding briskly into the room. 'There should be an empty bed for you in here.'

But there wasn't! A quick glance round showed that each of the eight beds was fully occupied. Mr Wilkins said: 'H'm, that's funny!' Then he went off to consult the dormitory list pinned on the noticeboard at the head of the stairs.

Sure enough, there was Blotwell's name listed for Dormitory 3, and a distinctly puzzled Mr Wilkins headed once again in that direction. On the way he passed Jennings hurrying towards Dormitory 6.

'Come along, Jennings, hurry up! It's time for lights out, and you're not undressed yet.'

'Sorry sir; shan't be a minute now, sir. Did you have a decent holiday sir?'

Mr Wilkins marched into Dormitory 3, determined at all costs to solve the mystery of the missing bed.

'Silence in here!' he commanded. 'All keep quiet while I check your names. There's been a mistake somewhere, and...'

At that moment, he glanced along the line of beds and noticed a vacant place in the middle. Jennings had smoothed the pillow and tidied the counterpane before leaving, and the bed showed no signs of having been used as a refuge for foreign agents.

'Who sleeps there?' demanded Mr Wilkins.

'Blotwell, sir,' said Thompson.

28

'Yes, but... I could have sworn someone was in there a few moments ago.'

Thompson jumped nimbly out of bed to investigate. 'There's no one here now, sir,' he said, searching beneath the pillow and peering down into the tunnel of bedclothes.

'Get back into bed, Thompson, you silly little boy! Of course there's no one in it now.'

'Would anyone mind if *I* got in then?' yawned Blotwell sleepily

Mr Wilkins called: 'Silence.' Then he made a round of the other dormitories to see that the occupants were properly bedded down. In Dormitory 6, he found Jennings sitting up in bed writing his diary 'Quickly now, Jennings, put that thing away. Time for lights out,' he said.

'Yes, sir. Just finishing off, sir. There's not much to write about the first day back at school, is there, sir?' Jennings said. 'No exciting mysteries, or anything like that.'

'Just as well there aren't,' Mr Wilkins answered shortly. 'This is a preparatory school, not a police station – and the fewer mysteries the better.'

He put out the light. All the same, he couldn't help pondering over the mystery of the bed in Dormitory 3. School life was like that, he thought, as he made his way downstairs to the staff room. In any other walk of life there would be some reasonable explanation of these fantastic mysteries that were always cropping up. But not at school... Oh, no!

Mr Wilkins stopped pondering as he reached the staff room door. By now, the strange case of the body in the bed had become just another of those riddles of school life to which there seemed to be no answer.

2

Top Secret

For the first week of the Easter term, Jennings found no difficulty in keeping his diary up to date. Every evening, just before bedtime, he would squat on the hot-water pipes in the tuck-box room, making notes on what he had eaten for lunch and recording the result of that afternoon's football game.

On Thursday Darbishire looked in to see how his friend was getting on, and was surprised to see that Jennings' forehead was ploughed with furrows of deep thought.

'What are you looking so fossilised about?' Darbishire inquired with kindly concern.

'I was just thinking,' replied Jennings, fidgeting uncomfortably on his over-heated perch. 'It's about my diary. I reckon I ought to *do* something about it.'

'There's nothing you *can* do with a diary, except write in it.' Darbishire smiled encouragingly 'Never mind, Jen, it's January twentieth already. Only another forty-nine weeks to New Year's Eve, and then you can stop. Good job it's not leap year. Three hundred and sixty-*five* days doesn't sound so bad; but three hundred and sixty-*six* Well, that'd be the last straw, wouldn't it!'

'It's not *that* I'm worried about; it's – well, you saw what happened in the dorm the other night. Dash it all, a diary's supposed to be private; but if ancient ruins like Venables and all that mob are going to keep poking their noses in, you might as well broadcast the thing on the six o'clock news.'

Jennings felt strongly on the matter. Keeping a diary for a whole year was not a task to be undertaken lightly. However, he had made the resolution and he was determined to carry it out. So far, it is true, the diary contained nothing of a confidential nature. The most recent entries read: *Wednesday: Had bath. We won, two-nil. Thursday: Had second helping of prunes, clean socks and French test. Friday: Broke bootlace.*

But after all, the year was young yet. Soon, no doubt, many pages would be covered with highly secret information.

'If only I could think of some way of doing it so no one else could read it,' said Jennings thoughtfully.

'Why not write it upside down,' suggested Darbishire. 'That ought to fox them all right.'

Jennings heaved an impatient sigh: 'Don't be so stark raving haywire! All they'd have to do would be to turn the book the other way up.'

Darbishire pursed his lips and stroked an imaginary beard – a device he had worked out in the holidays to help him to think more deeply. Rather to his surprise, it worked; for at once an idea sprang to his mind. 'I've got it,' he cried, his eyes lighting up with inspiration. 'Shorthand! Like that chap – what was his name? – that Mr Carter was telling us about last term. He kept a diary in shorthand.'

'Who – Mr Carter?'

'No, you clodpoll. Samuel Pepys – that's the chap. And after he was dead, it took some old professor years to work out what it was all about.'

But Darbishire's bright idea had to be rejected on practical grounds. As Jennings pointed out, it was necessary to know something about the subject before attempting to keep a diary in shorthand. What he needed was some ingenious, yet simple, code: some rearrangement of the written word that would baffle any unauthorised reader.

Jennings gazed round the room in search of inspiration. In front of him was a row of tuck-boxes, each bearing the name of the owner. Venables ... Atkinson ... Martin-Jones ... stood out in bold block letters. Almost without thinking, Jennings ran his eye along the painted names; then he read them backwards, and immediately he leaped to his feet and slapped his friend heartily between the shoulder blades.

'Wacko, I've got it, Darbi!' he cried excitedly '*Selbanev ... Nosnikta ... Senoj-Nitram.*'

'I beg your pardon?' queried Darbishire, out of his depth. He straightened his glasses, which had suffered during the back-slapping and were now athwart his nose like a percentage sign.

'*Selbanev, Nosnikta, Senoj-Nitram,*' Jennings repeated. 'They're the names of people, I bet you can't guess who!'

'Russian agents?... Zulu tribesmen?... Ancient kings of Egypt?' hazarded Darbishire.

'No, no, no,' Jennings flipped his fingers in delight and danced ungainly ballet steps round the tuck-boxes. 'Oh, wacko! If you can't guess, neither will anybody else, so we can use it for the code.'

Darbishire continued to brood over the problem. 'They must be foreigners of some sort,' he argued. 'You don't find names like that in the telephone directory. They aren't, er – spacemen from Mars or somewhere, I suppose?'

'No, you coot! I'll tell you, shall I? Venables, Atkinson and Martin-Jones spelt backwards.' Jennings ran his finger along the tuck-boxes from right to left, spelling out the names of the owners aloud.

'H'm. Not bad!' Darbishire agreed, as

light dawned. 'I see it now of course. Just the job for a diary. You could put in all sorts of things without anyone knowing what you were talking about. It'd be one in the eye for Venables, wouldn't it, if you wrote something like: *Selbanev is a clodpoll?* He'd never know it really meant him.'

Fired with enthusiasm, Jennings lost no time in trying out his code on the memoranda pages of his diary. He wrote *Selbanev si a llopdolc*; and then spent some time trying to read the last word aloud.

'Of course, it doesn't really matter whether you can pronounce the words, because they're only meant to be read,' he explained. 'Now, let's see what everybody else looks like in reverse gear.'

The work of research went forward. A few of the boys had names which, with a little imagination, could be spoken aloud when written in the code. *Elpmet* was a fairly easy word to pronounce when referring to Temple: *Snnib Ronim* could be rolled glibly off the tongue when Binns minor was the subject of discussion.

Other names needed more care. Darbishire spent some time mouthing *Erihsibrad* over and over again before he could pronounce his own name to his satisfaction. Jennings had even more trouble trying to say: 'My name is *Sgninnej*.' And when they tried, with reversed spellings, to talk about

35

Bromwich and Thompson, the air rang with guttural grunts and frog-like croaks.

'I shall only use the code for the private bits and chaps' names and things,' Jennings decided. 'I shan't bother to translate things like "swopped cheese labels", because there's nothing specially secret about that.' He sat down and started to compose an entry describing the events of that afternoon.

Darbishire went on experimenting. He tore an old luggage label from one of the tuck-boxes and translated Linbury Court Preparatory School into the new code. After some seconds of silent rehearsal, he spluttered: *'Y-rubnil Tru-oc Yrot-ara-perp Loohcs.'*

'Uh?' queried Jennings, looking up from his writing.

'That's the name of the school. Wouldn't it look smashing printed like that on headed notepaper! Our parents would think we'd moved to Yugoslavia or somewhere, when we wrote home on Sunday.'

He gurgled with laughter as his imagination painted a picture of the chaos and confusion that would result. 'They'd all copy the address on to the envelope when they wrote back, and nobody would...'

'Oh, don't be such a prehistoric ruin,' said Jennings impatiently. 'You know perfectly well it would never happen.'

'No, I suppose it wouldn't,' Darbishire

replied sadly, the little comedy fading from his mind. 'Still, there's no harm in just pretending. You need something to cheer you up after coping with Old Wilkie's maths lessons all day.'

The door of the tuck-box room swung open, and Mr Carter, the senior master, looked in. He was a friendly man, in his mid-thirties, who had spent so many years looking after boys that he knew more than most people about the workings of the eleven-year-old-mind. He was on duty that evening and, as usual, was making one of his systematic tours of the building to see how the boys were spending the half-hour before bedtime.

'I thought I'd find somebody down here,' Mr Carter said. 'It's a remarkable thing that although the headmaster provides you with a comfortable library and a well-stocked hobbies room, yet you prefer to spend your free time burrowing like moles round the hot-water pipes in the basement.'

'We were just working out a code for my diary, sir,' Jennings explained. 'You know, like Samuel Pepys – only different.'

'Yes, sir. Instead of shorthand, we're going to use a sort of back-to-front hand,' added Darbishire.

'Really!' marvelled Mr Carter.

'Yes, sir. I promised my Aunt Angela I wouldn't miss a day and I've kept it up jolly well, so far, sir. Would you like to see?' Jennings held the book out for the master's inspection.

'But isn't it private?' Mr Carter demurred.

'Parts of it are, sir. But all the private bits are going to be done in code, so you wouldn't be able to understand them. You see if you can, sir.'

'Yes, sir; it's ever so good. Try pitting your wits against it, sir.'

The two boys exchanged superior, knowing smiles, and stood back to follow the wit-pitting with quiet amusement. Theirs was a code ingenious enough to baffle the keenest of brains. Let Mr Carter puzzle it out – if he could!

The master strained his eyes over the spidery writing. *'Not so hot toddy,'* he read aloud, and added: 'You're quite safe, Jennings. I've no idea what that means.'

'Oh, but, sir, that part's not in code.' Jennings turned over the pages until he came to the sample he had just composed. 'There, sir. You just try reading that!'

Mr Carter read: *'Played football with Selbanev, Erihsibrad, Nosnikta and Co. Retsim Retrac reffed the game.* Sounds as though you were playing against the Moscow Dynamos,' he commented.

The boys flipped their fingers with delight.

'Don't you know who they are, sir? Oh, wacko!' crowed Jennings.

'Yes, of course, they're...' Mr Carter paused. He had been about to reel off the names of the people referred to, for the solution of the code had caused him little trouble. Then he had caught sight of the satisfied glow of triumph on the boys' faces: they were reaping so much enjoyment from the idea that their code was an unsolvable mystery that he decided not to guess the answer too quickly 'They are – er ... well, I should say these names refer to the members of some Eastern European spy organisation,' he said solemnly.

'No, sir. Wrong, sir!' Jennings bounced up and down on the hot pipes, while Darbishire subsided on to a tuck-box, hugging his knees to his chest in delight.

'I'll tell you, shall I, sir?' Jennings went on. 'It's secret really of course, but I don't mind you knowing, if you agree not to spread it around, sir.'

Mr Carter agreed.

'Well: *Selbanev* is Venables the wrong way round, and *Nosnikta* is Atkinson in reverse.'

'I see,' said Mr Carter. 'And who is this mysterious *Retsim Retrac* who reffed the game?'

'That's you, sir ... Mister Carter, sir!'

'Fancy that!' marvelled the new-styled Retsim Retrac. He gave the little red book back to the smiling owner. 'All the same, Jennings, I suggest you worry less about your code, and more about your style of writing. Those entries are hardly in the Samuel Pepys tradition.'

'I know, sir, but what else can I put? That's the trouble with boarding school – you get the same old things happening every day.' He slipped the diary in his pocket. 'I bet Samuel Pepys would have got fed up, just writing down football results and things, sir.'

The discussion was interrupted by the ringing of the dormitory bell. It was a pity Jennings thought, as he trotted up the stairs, that Samuel Pepys was dead; he sounded just the sort of chap who would have been interested to hear of this modern improvement on the seventeenth-century method of keeping a secret diary.

When they reached the dormitory, Darbishire said: 'If you want to be really up to date, Jen, you could write your tomorrow's news bulletin tonight. I know what's going to happen.'

'So do I: another of Mr Wilkins' ghastly history tests.'

'Yes, but that's not all. Old Wilkie's threatened to go into a roof-level attack on anyone who doesn't get full marks, so we'd better look out!'

3

Jennings Finds an Ally

Mr Wilkins strode briskly into Form 3 classroom, his eyes glowing with enthusiasm for the day's work ahead.

'Everybody ready for the test?' he boomed. 'Right! First question – write down the date…'

'Oh, sir, wait a minute, sir! Not so fast, please sir!' Form 3 protested, searching feverishly for pens and blotting paper.

'Hurry up, hurry up! Question *One* for the last time: write down the date…'

'Yes, sir, I've done that,' Darbishire announced brightly. 'I've written the date, sir.'

Mr Wilkins looked at him sharply. 'Don't be stupid, Darbishire. I haven't told you yet which date I want you to write.'

'Oh, sorry, sir; I thought you meant today's date.'

The enthusiastic glow began to fade from Mr Wilkins' eyes. Patiently he said: 'Question *One* is the date of the Battle of Bannockburn. Question *Two*…'

Jennings sat in the back row, his head

propped in his hands. He had awakened with a headache that morning and was feeling far from well. At breakfast he had toyed with his food, unable to face his favourite menu of bacon and fried bread; and now Mr Wilkins' vast voice and heavy footsteps were making him feel a lot worse.

Why, he wondered, did Mr Wilkins find it necessary to stamp around the room like a drill squad marking time in army boots? Why must he announce each question in the tones of a sea captain encouraging his crew in the teeth of a booming gale?

Jennings began to wish that he had gone to see Matron after breakfast. She was an understanding sort of person who knew at once when people would be better off in bed than facing the rigours of a history test.

Too late, of course, to report now, for Mr Wilkins was rattling out question after question as though taking part in some historical speed trial. Jennings pulled himself together and reached for his pen – only to find that it had mysteriously disappeared. That's funny, he thought; he was almost sure he had left it on his desk... Sabotage, perhaps! He raised his hand.

'Sir, please sir, I haven't got a pen.'

Mr Wilkins paused in the middle of announcing a new question, a frown of annoyance gathering on his brow, 'Do it in pencil, then.' he said curtly 'Next question...

Well, what is it *now*, Jennings?'

'Please, sir, I haven't got a pencil, either.'

'I... I... Corwumph!' said Mr Wilkins. It really was too bad! Here they were, halfway through the questions and...! 'Go and borrow a pencil, Jennings, and hurry up about it.'

Mr Wilkins watched with mounting impatience as Jennings started off on a leisurely tour of the classroom. 'Got a pencil to lend, Atkinson?' he inquired.

'No, sorry.'

'How about you, Venables?'

'No good; I'm using mine.'

Jennings passed on from desk to desk without success, while Mr Wilkins tapped his foot and drummed on his mark book with restless fingers. Finally he could stand it no longer.

'Oh, for goodness' sake! You're holding up the whole class. Who can lend this wretched boy a pencil?'

'I can, sir,' volunteered Bromich major from the far end of the room.

'Well, why didn't you say so before? You can see I'm in a hurry to get on.'

'He hasn't asked me yet, sir. I was just waiting till he'd worked his way round to my desk.'

At last Jennings returned to his place. Mr Wilkins took a deep breath. Now, perhaps, he could proceed with the lesson.

'Next question,' he announced. 'What was the date of...?'

'Oh, sir, please sir.'

But Jennings hand was up again.

'I... I... What on earth is it this time, boy?'

'Please, sir, may I borrow a penknife, sir? I've just broken the point.'

'Doh!' An explosive sound like the bursting of a toy balloon, detonated its way through Mr Wilkins' vocal chords. He clasped one hand over his eyes, while the other thumped a tattoo of exasperation on the master's desk.

It is not surprising that Jennings failed to do well in the history test. His headache grew worse, and, even if he had had a pencil with a point, it is doubtful whether he would have been able to do himself justice. As it was, he failed to achieve the pass mark, and his name was entered in the punishment book for an hour's detention during football that afternoon.

'And what's more, Jennings, you'll stay in until you know the work properly. If you haven't learnt it by teatime, you'll come back and do it again afterwards.'

'Yes, sir,' said Jennings.

The prospect of missing football did not worry him, for he was not feeling well enough to play. All he wanted to do was to go to bed. At last the bell rang for the end of the lesson, and Jennings found himself surrounded by a group of boys, some anxious to sympathise, others eager to gloat over his misfortune.

'Bad luck, Jennings,' Darbishire consoled him. 'Can't be helped, though: it was just hard cheese that Old Wilkie happened to be in one of his moods.'

'It's your own fault for holding up the whole class,' said Temple righteously. 'If you want to know what *I* think, you jolly well deserved to be kept in during football.'

'I shan't be here this afternoon,' Jennings answered. 'I'm feeling rotten. I'm going up to ask Matron if I can go to bed.'

A hoot of derision arose from the ranks of the gloaters.

'Hear that? He's trying to get out of Old Wilkie's punishment. You bogus swizzler, Jennings – there's nothing the matter with you.'

'Yes there is, then. I've got a headache.'

'Huh! Prove, it,' demanded Temple, in tones of scathing disbelief. 'I bet you can't prove it.'

'Of course I can't. You don't *have* to prove things like that.' Jennings turned and groped his way out of the room with his hand over his eyes. Perhaps *that* would show these heartless scoffers how ill he really felt!

However, it didn't. For Mr Wilkins, drinking tea in the staff room, overheard a high-pitched news bulletin being broadcast in the passage beyond the door.

'I say have you heard? Jennings is faking a headache so he can back out of a punishment this afternoon.'

'No!'

'Yes, honestly! He's gone to the sickroom. Of course, there's nothing wrong with him really. Wouldn't Old Wilkie be livid if he knew it was just a put-up job!'

Mr Wilkins frowned thoughtfully at his teacup. So that was the game, was it! Very well, he'd soon show small boys that they couldn't take liberties with *him*. He put down his cup and strode off to the sickroom with a purposeful tread.

When he arrived, he found Jennings sitting on a chair near the door, sucking a clinical thermometer. Matron was busy pouring out medicine at the far end of the room.

'Now, what is all this nonsense about, Jennings?' demanded Mr Wilkins, briskly.

Jennings looked up, uncertain whether or not to answer. Matron had told him to sit still and not talk while his temperature was being taken. On the other hand, one couldn't remain dumb when questioned by a master. He pointed at the little glass tube and muttered guttural grunts through closed lips.

'What?'

It was Matron who came to Jennings'

rescue by hurrying forward in defence of her patient. 'You mustn't talk to him now, Mr Wilkins,' she said. 'If he tries to answer, he'll probably bite through the thermometer.'

Jennings liked Matron. She was young and friendly – the sort of person to whom one could always turn in time of crisis. Moreover, she had a flair for detecting whether any complaint of ill-health was genuine or bogus. One glance at Jennings' flushed cheeks and dull eyes had told her that the boy was far from feeling his usual bright self.

'I can't see any point in taking his temperature,' grumbled Mr Wilkins. 'It's obvious that there's nothing whatever the matter with him.'

Matron smiled. 'That's for me to decide,' she replied. 'In any case, I shan't be sending him down to school again today.'

'You won't! But he's got to go into my detention class this afternoon.'

It was not a matter that could be discussed in front of the patient, so Matron took Mr Wilkins into her sitting-room, across the passage. What she said, Jennings didn't know; but, even though he had no intention of listening, he could hardly help hearing Mr Wilkins' booming answers.

'It's ridiculous, Matron,' the master was protesting. 'Everybody knows the boy is just trying it on. It was hearing the rest of his form laughing about it that made me decide to look into the matter.'

There followed a pause while Matron replied. Then Mr Wilkins, his voice raised in annoyance, said: 'Oh! Well, all I can say is, Matron, I am surprised that a person of your experience should be so easily hoodwinked by an eleven-year-old boy.'

The door banged, and Mr Wilkins' heavy footfall gradually receded along the corridor. Next moment, Matron was back in the sickroom with her patient.

'You do really *believe* I'm not feeling well, don't you?' Jennings said.

'Yes, of course I do.'

'Have I got a temp.?' he asked, as she took the thermometer from him.

She narrowed her eyes to read the fine column of mercury.

'Yes, you have, Jennings, but not a very high one. You're probably a little bilious; you'll be as right as a trivet tomorrow.'

'Don't I have to go back into school today, then?'

'Certainly not. Go to your dormitory and get into bed; I'll come along later and have another look at you.'

Jennings was deeply impressed by the way Matron had defended him against the wrath of Mr Wilkins. Good old Matron; she was ever so decent, he thought, as he climbed into bed. Just as well that he *had* got a temperature, all things considered. He would have let her down badly if the thermometer had pronounced him normal.

He lay in bed wondering how best he could repay her act of kindness. Perhaps he would buy her a present...Yes, that was it! A really expensive present. In a sudden glow of generosity he made up his mind to spend the whole of the five shillings which his Uncle Arthur had given him the day he returned to school. He would buy her ... well, *something* anyway. Tomorrow, when he was feeling better, he would discuss the matter with Darbishire to see whether he had any bright ideas on the subject. For the moment, he would just make a note in his diary to buy something for Matron ... a private note, of course, for this was a secret matter, worthy to be written in code,

He wrote: '*Yub gnihtemos rof Nortam*,' and then lay down with closed eyes to ease his aching head.

By the evening, Jennings was feeling better, and was sitting up in bed tying bowlines with his dressing-gown cord when the other boys arrived in the dormitory.

'Huh! So you're still alive, then!' Temple greeted him.

'Yes, I'm much better, thanks. Decent of you to inquire after my health. Matron says I'll be as right as a trivet by the morning.'

'What's a trivet?' demanded Temple suspiciously. It sounded to him like some new dodge to avoid going back into school.

'A trivet? Well, it's – er, something that tells you how right people are. It's like being as right as rain, or...'

'My father says you're as right as ninepence,' Darbishire chimed in.

'Then your father must be crazy! How can Jennings be as right as ninepence, if he's been in bed all day with a temperature?' said Atkinson.

'No, he doesn't mean *Jennings* is as right as ninepence...' Darbishire began.

'You just said he did.'

'I mean my father would be able to say so tomorrow, when Jennings is better.'

'How's he going to know that? He lives a hundred miles away.'

'Oh, shut up, all of you!' cried Jennings. 'Here am I, supposed to be an invalid recovering from a temperature, and everyone keeps nattering about my being right as ninepence. It's enough to give me a relapse.'

The following afternoon, Matron allowed him to get up. She would not permit him to play football, so he wandered down to the changing-room to talk to Darbishire, whom he found struggling into his football jersey in readiness for the afternoon's game.

'Listen, Darbi; Matron's been jolly decent to me,' Jennings began. 'She came to my rescue like a house on fire when Old Wilkie had me in his gun sights yesterday morning.'

'I expect he'll be on the prowl again, now you're better,' Darbishire observed gloomily 'You'll want to watch your step with Mr Wilkins till he cools off a bit.'

But Jennings was too full of praise for Matron to bother about Mr Wilkins. 'I'm going to give her a present as a reward,' he said. 'Something decent, of course. What can you buy for five shillings?'

Darbishire considered. 'A driving licence,' he suggested brightly.

'That's no good; she hasn't got a car.'

'Or you could buy two half-crown books of stamps, or twenty threepenny slabs of chocolate or...'

'Oh, don't talk such dehydrated bilge-water,' Jennings complained. 'What would Matron want with all that chocolate?'

'I never said she *would* want it. You asked me what cost five shillings, and I said...'

'All right. Let's not go through it all over again. I only asked because I thought you might like to come and help choose it. We could get permission from Mr Carter to go into Linbury after lunch next Wednesday, and see if they've got anything decent in the village shop.'

His friend nodded in agreement. 'Suits me; I don't mind coming along and giving a spot of advice in a good cause.'

The prospect of helping to spend five shillings of someone else's money was a pleasant one. But it is doubtful whether Darbishire would have felt quite so pleased, if he had been able to foresee what the expedition held in store for him.

4

The Scarlet Runner

The village of Linbury has one serious disadvantage when considered as a flourishing shopping centre: it has no flourishing shops. There are, it is true, three establishments where odd purchases may be made, but none of them caters for the keen buyer of personal gifts with five shillings to spend.

Jennings and Darbishire made this discovery soon after they reached the village on the following Wednesday afternoon. First, they pressed their noses to the plate glass window of *H Higgins, Jeweller & Silversmith*; and were disappointed in his stock of tarnished watch chains and flyblown sugar tongs. A notice offering to engrave dog collars within forty-eight hours offered them little encouragement, so they wandered into the *Linbury Stores and Post Office* farther down the street.

Here the range, though wider, was equally useless, for it consisted mainly of household goods, such as bird seed, corn plasters, galvanised-iron buckets and brussels sprouts.

'This is hopeless,' Jennings complained, running his eye round the displays of tinned peas and soap flakes. 'There's nothing here she'd want.'

'What about a pot-scourer or one of those egg timers?' suggested Darbishire.

'No good at all. You can't give anyone an egg timer unless you give them an egg to go with it, and we'd probably bust it before we got it back to school.'

Then Darbishire discovered a patent folding tin-opener, and spent some time opening it to see how it worked.

'How about this, then?' he asked. 'Jolly useful for opening things. It's on a spring, look, and it snaps shut like... Ow!'

He broke off suddenly and went for a short walk round the shop, with his body bent double and his hands clasped between his knees. When he returned, he said: 'I don't think I should buy one of those, Jennings; they're dangerous. They don't give your knuckles time to get out of the way.'

The assistant behind the post-office counter looked up from her stamps. 'Anything I can get you?' she inquired.

'No thanks; we're just looking round,' Jennings said, and hurriedly led the way outside.

As the shop door shut behind them, Darbishire massaged his bruised knuckles and said: 'I suppose we'll just have to call the whole thing off, then. There's nowhere else we can try.'

But Jennings was frowning thoughtfully at a notice painted on a board in a cottage window a few yards farther along the street: *Chas Lumley – Homemade Cakes and Bicycles Repaired.* 'What about trying there?' he suggested.

'No wizard fear! That's the place where Venables took us to tea last term, and then found he'd left his money at home.' Darbishire shivered slightly at the embarrassing memory. 'I'm not going in there again in a hurry. Besides, they only sell doughnuts and things, and you couldn't give Matron a plate full of those for a present.'

'You can hire bikes there as well,' Jennings pointed out.

'Yes, but would Matron want a bicycle ride? Sounds a feeble sort of present to me.'

Jennings continued to stare at the notice for a few seconds more. Then he turned to his friend, his eyes shining with inspiration. 'I've got it, Darbi! We can hire bikes at this place and cycle on to Dunhambury. There are masses of shops to choose from, there.'

The more Jennings thought about his scheme, the better he liked it. The market town of Dunhambury with its wide range of shops, lay a further four miles or so along the road from the village – barely twenty minutes by bicycle. If they started at once they would have ample time for their shopping expedition, for they were not due back at school for well over an hour. There was, unfortunately one serious snag, and Darbishire was quick to spot it.

'We're not allowed into Dunhambury without special permission,' he objected. 'And what's more, I bet we're not allowed to hire bikes, either.'

'But this is something special,' Jennings argued. 'Chaps don't buy presents for matrons every day of the week. I bet you what you like Mr Carter would have said it was all right, if we'd asked him.'

'Well, why didn't you ask him?'

Jennings clicked his teeth with impatience. 'I didn't know then that I'd want to go farther than the village. Anyway I've never heard a rule about not hiring bikes, so that proves there probably isn't one.'

Darbishire was not convinced by this last argument. He pointed out, for example, that he had never heard a school rule forbidding boys to keep man-eating crocodiles in the tuck-box room. All the same, he fancied the headmaster might raise some objection if anyone actually took advantage of this legal loophole.

'Don't be such a ruin,' Jennings complained. 'Here am I planning a supersonic bike-hiring scheme, and you have to start bishing up the issue with man-eating crocodiles. And I'll tell you another thing I've just thought of: some of the day boys, like Marshall and Pettigrew, come to school on bikes every day. So if it's all right for day boys, why not for boarders?'

Darbishire shrugged his shoulders. He knew it was useless to go on arguing when Jennings had made up his mind. With some misgiving he followed his friend through the gate and up the path to the little cycle shed at the top of the garden.

A stout man in shirt sleeves was coaxing a tyre on to a bicycle wheel. He looked up as the boys approached.

'Good afternoon! Are you Chas Lumley, Esq.?' Jennings asked.

The stout man admitted his identity with a grunt.

'Well, can you possibly let us have two bicycles until just before four o'clock, please?'

Mr Lumley rubbed his nose thoughtfully with a tyre lever, and said that such a thing might be arranged. It was a long time since anyone had hired one of his bicycles. Trade was not brisk in Linbury; and this was not surprising, for any luckless cyclist who had once spent an uncomfortable afternoon astride one of Mr Lumley's saddles was not likely to repeat the experience, if he could help it.

He went inside the shed and reappeared a

few moments later wheeling two cumbrous, old-fashioned bicycles. 'A shilling each, till four o'clock,' he said.

Jennings' spirits sank at the sight of his mount. It was the tallest, heaviest and most antiquated assortment of mobile iron-mongery that he had ever seen. As he stood beside it, the saddle reached as high as his chest, and the handlebars seemed to tower up into the air like a stag's antlers. The machine had been involved in an accident at some stage of its long life, and the front mudguard was now as puckered as a piefrill. The rear wheel, he observed, was fitted with a dress-guard, designed to prevent the loose-flowing garments of a previous era from catching in the spokes.

'Wow! What a chronic old rattletrap!' Jennings exclaimed. With a half-hearted attempt at humour, he turned to Mr Lumley and added: 'At any rate, I shouldn't think it will be too small for me.'

Mr Lumley seldom appreciated humour, half-hearted or otherwise. 'Plenty big enough,' he agreed solemnly. 'You won't need to higher the saddle on this machine.'

'Not hire the saddle!' Jennings stared at him in puzzled wonder. Surely the saddle was included. Was he expected to sit on the cross bar all afternoon?

'I think he means you won't need the saddle any higher,' Darbishire interpreted.

'I should jolly well think not. I shall need a turntable ladder to get aboard as it is.'

Jennings turned again to Mr Lumley. 'You haven't got anything just a little smaller, have you?'

But Mr Lumley hadn't. Muttering to himself, he set to work with hammer and spanner and lowered both saddles as far as they would go.

Behind the barrage of hammering, Darbishire whispered: 'I say, Jen, let's tell him we don't want them. We'll never get to Dunhambury on those old boneshakers.'

'We wizard well *will!*' Jennings maintained. 'Don't be so fussy Darbi; you can't expect streamlined jet-propelled models for a shilling. Besides, we can't back out now that the man's been to all that trouble to make them comfortable for us.'

Panting with his exertions, Mr Lumley finished his task. 'There you are. Reliable bikes, these! Nice comfortable seats, too.'

By way of demonstration, he gave the saddle of the nearer machine a resounding smack: an unwise move, as it happened, for one of the pedals immediately dropped off, and more time was wasted before the machine could again be pronounced roadworthy.

The cost of the hire had to be paid in advance, so Jennings handed over two of the shillings he had earmarked for Matron's present. Then the boys took hold of the handlebars and trundled their creaking vehicles on to the road.

'I vote we don't get on just yet. Let's wheel them round the corner into the lane,' Darbishire suggested.

'Why?' queried Jennings, impatient to be on his way.

'Well, er – I'm fond of walking; and besides there are too many people about for my liking,' Darbishire admitted uneasily.

'But we can't afford to pay good money for bikes, just to take them for a walk.'

'Only to the next corner. I'll have a bash at getting on then – honestly I will.'

Reluctantly Jennings agreed; and together they pushed their machines into the narrow lane where they could mount in privacy.

From the outset it was clear that the journey would be a noisy one. Jennings' bicycle had a loose mudguard-stay which caught in the spokes every time the wheel went round. At slow speeds it emitted a deep musical *doyng-a-doyng* like the G string of a 'cello; and as the machine went faster the note rose up the scale and wailed like a siren. There was also a soft, rhythmic *plonk* which was caused by the fact that the wheel was no longer the perfect circle that it had been twenty years before.

Darbishire's bicycle, also, gave audible warning of its approach. Both the cranks were bent inwards and knocked against the flapping gear case at each revolution of the pedals. The near-side crank sounded a high-pitched *ker-pink,* while its neighbour was content to throb out a bass *ker-tumf.* Other parts of the machine added squeaks and rattles in various keys. The only really silent feature was the bell, but this was hardly noticeable amongst the general volume of sound.

Doyng-a-doyng-a...plonk!... *Doyng-a-doyng-a...plonk!* sang Jennings' back wheel.

Ker-tumf... Ker-pink!... Ker-tumf... Ker-pink! answered Darbishire's gear case.

As soon as they were round the corner, Jennings scooted along on one pedal, swung his leg high into the air and gained the saddle with an effort.

'This is smashing, isn't it, Darbi!' he called gaily 'We'll be there in two shakes of a lamb's tail.' He glanced back over his shoulder and noticed that his friend was still plodding along on foot.

'Well, get cracking, Darbishire! You're not on a walking tour.'

'Don't worry about me. I'm not quite ready to get on yet,' said Darbishire apologetically.

Jennings sensed that all was not well. He dismounted and waited for his friend to catch him up. 'What's the trouble?' he asked.

Darbishire looked uncomfortable. 'I can't ride the thing,' he confessed sadly. 'I can only ride low bicycles. I shall never be able to manage a ghastly old fire-escape like this.'

'You can't ride it!' Jennings was aghast.

'No, I haven't done much cycling. You see, the traffic's rather heavy where we live, and my father says I'm only allowed to ride...'

'But, you great, prehistoric clodpoll, Darbi!' Jennings stormed. 'If you can't ride the thing, why on earth didn't you say so before I forked out a large chunk of Matron's money to pay for it?'

'I did. I said let's not bother, but you wouldn't listen.'

They stood glaring at each other over the crossbars; Jennings exasperated beyond measure, Darbishire resentful and unhappy Finally Darbishire gave in.

'Well, I'll have a bash then, considering it's for Matron's benefit, but you'll have to hold the thing steady while I climb aboard, because I can't reach the pedals when they're down at the bottom.'

If only Mr Lumley had tightened the nuts properly after lowering the saddle, it is just possible that Darbishire might have been able to sit astride the machine without swivelling round like a rotating gun-turret. Unfortunately it was not until he was in position that he discovered this flaw in the seating arrangements.

Jennings gave the bicycle a push to start it on its way and Darbishire pressed down hard on the near-side pedal. As he did so, the saddle tilted over at a sharp angle and swung round in a semicircle. The machine lurched crazily as the rider sought to regain control. Then the off-side pedal rose to the top of its circuit, and Darbishire gave it a jab with his right foot as it went past. Immediately, the saddle responded to this change of balance, veered round from east to west and developed an alarming list to starboard.

'Sit up straight,' advised Jennings from behind.

'I can't – it won't let me.' Darbishire would gladly have dismounted if only he could have reached either pedal at the bottom of its stroke; but, as this was out of the question, he wobbled on down the road, kicking the pedals round whenever he could reach them and swaying on his free-swinging saddle in wide, uncontrollable arcs.

'Jolly good, keep it going!' Jennings jumped on his machine and soon caught up with his floundering companion. For twenty yards the bicycles ran side by side *ker-tumf*-ing, *ker-pink*-ing and *doyng-a-doyng-a-plonk*-ing like a percussion band duet.

But the effort of steering under these conditions was too much for Darbishire.

Before he quite knew what had happened, the handlebars had swivelled round towards the hedge, the front wheel had hit the bank, and the rider found himself lying on the grass with his machine on top of him.

'Hurt yourself?' asked Jennings, dismounting for the second time.

Darbishire straightened his glasses and scrambled to his feet. 'No, I'm all right – so far. It's that crazy saddle; it jerks you about like a bucking broncho. It's all very well for chaps in the Boat Race to have sliding seats, but it's a bit thick to fix them on bikes.'

He heaved the machine on to its wheels and pointed to his troublesome perch which had now swung full circle and was pointing over the rear mudguard. 'Dash it all, Jen, I shall never know whether I'm going or coming on this old bone-shaker. We'll have to take it back and let the man fix it again.'

Jennings smote his crossbar with frustration. 'But we *can't*, Darbi – we haven't time. It's nearly three o'clock already and we haven't started yet. You'll just have to make the best of it.'

'I'm not riding this bike till someone stops the saddle flapping about like a weather-cock,' said Darbishire stubbornly. 'I'd rather push the thing all the way to Dunhambury and back.'

'All right then; you can jolly well go ahead and push it.'

'No, you go ahead,' Darbishire amended. 'I'll come on behind as fast as I can.'

It was an ill-equipped pair of travellers who set out along the Dunhambury road. First came Jennings, towering as high as the hedge top as he clanked and rattled his way along. Behind him ran Darbishire, trundling his cumbersome vehicle along at full gallop, and scarlet in the face with his exertions. His forehead was damp with perspiration, his tie was slewed round beneath his left ear, and his socks were hanging concertina-fashion about his ankles. 'If only Jennings wouldn't go so fast' he thought bitterly as he lumbered along, losing ground every second, but determined not to be left behind.

At that moment, Jennings called over his shoulder: 'Come on, Darbi, run up! You can't expect me to crawl along at four miles a fortnight just because of you.'

'Phew! Not so fast – I shall burst!' gasped Darbishire. They were climbing a hill now and the going was heavy. Jennings glanced back and the sight of his struggling friend made him laugh so much that he was in danger of losing his balance.

'You do look funny Darbi, tanking along at full pelt, shoving that old rattletrap.'

'Well, *you* get off and walk, too. It wouldn't look so funny if we were both walking.'

'No fear, I'm enjoying my ride.'

Fortunately for Darbishire, the slope grew

steeper as the road wound past the site of an old Roman encampment. Soon Jennings dismounted, unable to pedal his heavy machine against the gradient.

'Phew, thank goodness!' panted Darbishire. 'I've had enough of pushing this old mangle. There's something catching in the back wheel all the time. It's started to tick now, as well as making all those other noises.' He stopped to investigate the cause of the trouble. 'It's my back brake block – it's broken,' he announced.

'That's difficult to say isn't it?' said Jennings. 'My black brake brock's broken... No, that's wrong... My brack blake bock's bloken... Oh, never mind. We're nearly at the top of the hill now; then, I'm going to ride again.'

'Oh no, Jen, don't be a cad! I'm too puffed,' Darbishire protested. 'My breathing apparatus hasn't sprung back into shape yet.'

Jennings glanced at his watch; it was getting late. Too much time had been lost already. 'Sorry, Darbi, you'll just have to put up with it. We'll never get to Dunhambury on bicycles if we walk.'

Darbishire sighed. Things were not going very well; but worse was to follow before the afternoon was over.

5

So Long at the Fair

As the boys reached the top of the hill, the raucous sound of mechanical music blared down the road to meet them: on a patch of waste ground a short distance ahead, they could see the marquees, caravans and swing boats of a travelling fair.

At once, Darbishire forgot his weariness. 'Come on, Jennings; let's go and have a look. We needn't stay long.'

'We mustn't stay at all, or we shan't get to Dunhambury before lighting-up time,' Jennings answered.

All the same, the temptation to stop for a few moments and explore the garish attractions of the fairground was strong. Surely there could be no harm in having just one quick look! They need not – in fact they *must* not – spend any money for the hiring of the bicycles had already made drastic inroads into the five shillings ear-marked for Matron's present. That had been unavoidable, of course, for without transport there could *be* no present. But not a penny must be spent on selfish pleasure!

They hurried along the road; Jennings riding again now, while Darbishire panted along behind, sometimes running, sometimes scooting on one pedal.

It was only a small fair, in spite of the fact that *Mummery's Mammoth Amusements* was inscribed in large letters on a banner which fluttered over the entrance to the waste ground.

The wording of the banner puzzled Darbishire. 'What's a mammoth amusement?' he inquired with interest.

'I don't know. Perhaps they've got a zoo with a mammoth in it,' Jennings guessed.

'Surely not! You don't find mammoths anywhere these days. They're defunct, like dodos and hippogriffs and things.'

'Well, they must have got one or they wouldn't say so. Let's go in and see if we can see it anywhere.'

They felt quite safe in parking their bicycles by the roadside; no thief would get far on either of *those* derelict machines! Then they hurried inside to inspect the mammoth amusements.

They were not disappointed. There was no sign of the mammoth, but the roundabout was excitingly furnished with miniature tanks and jet aircraft.

'Wacko, how smashing!' crowed Jennings, hopping from foot to foot in joyous anticipation. 'We *must* have a go on that, Darbi.

You could have a tank, and I could come behind you in a jet fighter and shoot you up, as we go round.'

'Coo, yes! And I could pot back at you with that twelve pounder sticking out of the...' Darbishire broke off suddenly. His face fell. 'But we can't, can we? I mean – what about Matron's present?'

Jennings hesitated. Two sixpenny tickets on the roundabout would still leave him with two shillings. Surely that would be enough for their purpose! Why in a place like Dunhambury there must be hundreds of acceptable gifts for that price. 'We'll just have one ride – definitely no more,' he said.

The roundabout came to a standstill and the two boys hopped eagerly aboard. Jennings lowered himself into his tiny cockpit and adjusted an imaginary flying helmet and goggles: Darbishire squeezed into a single-seater tank.

At once a desperate battle broke out between Fighter Command and Tank Corps. Crouching low in cockpit and gun-turret, the opposing forces hissed and snorted a fusillade of imaginary ammunition through clenched teeth. The barrage was deafening, as the sound of machine-gun fire rattled through vocal chords, and atom bombs exploded with deep, throat-clearing detonations.

'Hey what's going on?' demanded the

owner of the roundabout, popping his head out from behind the steam-organ to see what all the noise was about. He must have borne a charmed life, for he appeared unharmed by the spattering of ammunition bursting around him.

'Just having a friendly battle – nothing serious,' Jennings explained, as he handed over the money for the ride. Then, as the roundabout started to move, hostilities burst out again, and the tumult of war was added to the blaring din of the mechanical organ.

The ride was over all too soon; and the boys were so hoarse and so breathless after it, that they had to go and buy a bottle of lemonade apiece. Then they thought of the journey ahead, and of how ravenous they would be by the time they got back to school. So they staved off the pangs of hunger with a packet of potato crisps.

'We mustn't spend any more on ourselves,' said Jennings firmly, when the crisps had all gone. 'Every penny we've got left has got to go on Matron's present.'

'How much *have* we got left?' Darbishire asked.

'Oh, quite a bit. We haven't spent much really.' Jennings delved into his pocket, and immediately a look of alarm and despondency spread over his features. 'Fossilised fish-hooks,' he gasped in horror. 'I've only got sixpence left!'

'What! But we've hardly spent anything.'

'See for yourself, then.' Jennings waved the remaining coin under Darbishire's nose, and went on in a worried tone: 'I can't think where it's all gone. Surely we haven't spent all *that* much!'

But a simple calculation showed that they *had*. The hire of the bicycles, the ride on the roundabouts, the lemonade and potato crisps accounted for four and sixpence. Without realising their danger, they had became victims of that distressing complaint known as 'shortage of cash.'

'What can we do?' moaned Darbishire. 'We can't buy a decent present with only sixpence. Gosh, how mouldy! All that dosh to start with, and now we've only sixpence.'

'Only sixpence…! Only sixpence!'

Away to their left, a hoarse voice was shouting the phrase as though in echo. The boys turned and saw a flashily dressed showman in a vivid tie and heavily-padded shoulders standing beside a gaudy rifle range which bore the name: *Texas Dan's Wild West Commando Crackshots*. The show-man was shouting himself red in the face in his efforts to attract the attention of the crowd.

'Three shots for sixpence… Three shots for sixpence. Luverly prizes!' bawled Texas Dan, waving two airguns above his head like semaphore flags.

The boys strolled over to the rifle range to take a closer look at this Wild West Commando with smooth-creamed hair and patent leather shoes. They saw that the targets consisted of a number of clay pipes: any marksman, it seemed, who smashed one of these was entitled to choose his prize from the assortment of picture frames, garden gnomes, cut-glass vases and sticks of Brighton rock which were carefully stacked out of the line of fire.

'Come along, roll up!... Now's your chance to win a prize! Three shots for a tanner!'

'Wow! I'd like to have a bash with one of those airguns,' said Jennings.

Darbishire was shocked. 'But what about Matron? We came out specially for her sake.'

'I know, but how can we possibly buy her anything decent for sixpence? Don't think I'm not upset about it, Darbi, because I *am*. All the same it's no good crying over spilt milk, so I might just as well spend my last sixpence on this.'

Texas Dan had already sized Jennings up as a likely customer, and was thrusting an airgun towards him. 'Here you are, son! Now's your chance to have a crack on the genuine *Wild West Commando Range*.'

A moment later, sixpence had changed hands, and Jennings was squinting along the barrel of the airgun. There was a loud *phut* as he fired – but that was all!

'Bad luck,' sympathised Darbishire. 'I think that one went too high.'

'Keep quiet, Darbi. I can't aim properly with you chuntering away in the background,' the marksman complained.

But Jennings fared no better at his second attempt; and as he stood poised for his last shot, his finger tightening on the trigger, Darbishire suddenly exclaimed: 'I say Jennings, mind out...!'

The barrel waved wildly at this sudden interruption, and the gun went off before Jennings could steady his aim. Angrily he rounded on his friend. 'Now look what you've made me do! What did you want to butt in and make me waste my last shot for?'

'Sorry,' mumbled Darbishire. 'I was only going to say mind out you don't hit the prizes by mistake. Still I needn't have bothered, because you sent that last shot *bang-slap* on the target.'

Jennings turned back and glanced with surprise at the rows of clay pipes. Sure enough, the pipe on the extreme left was lying shattered in a dozen pieces: which was odd because he'd been aiming at the one on the *right!*

'Oh, wacko!' he crowed. 'Thanks very much Darbi. If you hadn't put me off, I shouldn't have been anywhere near the target area at all.'

The showman waved a pudgy hand at the stack of prizes. 'What are you going to have, son? Cut-glass vase? Genuine imitation pearl necklace?... Take your choice.'

Jennings frowned hard at the prizes, wondering which to choose. He had almost decided to ask for a stick of Brighton rock, when a much better idea flashed into his mind... He would choose something for Matron! Of course! It was the answer to his problem... 'I'll have one of those cut-glass vases, please,' he said.

Darbishire gave him a puzzled look; he had been hoping for Brighton rock. 'You're bats! What on earth do you want a cut-glass vase for?' he demanded.

'It's not for me – it's for Matron,' Jennings explained, as he took possession of his prize. 'Now I can give her a present after all.'

'Yes, of course. Jolly good wheeze! Shall I carry it for you? I'll be ever so careful.'

Darbishire was allowed to carry the gift which he squeezed into the pocket of his raincoat. Then they made their way back to the bicycles. It was getting late now – much later than they realised, for they had lost count of time while exploring the excitements of the fair.

Jennings glanced at his watch. 'Oh fish-hooks! It's half-past three,' he cried, in sudden panic. 'We'll have to pedal like blinko to get back to school by four o'clock. We've got to take the bikes back first, don't forget.'

'But I *can't* pedal like blinko on that old gridiron,' Darbishire pointed out. 'You seem to forget I'm doing my cycling on foot this afternoon.'

'You'll jolly well *have* to ride back, Darbi. There's no time for anything else. Try sitting on the crossbar, if the saddle swivels about too much.'

Doubt and distress were written on Darbishire's features as he heaved his machine to an upright position and mounted from the bank. He was not looking forward to the return journey. Glumly he set off, perched uncomfortably on the crossbar.

When they had pedalled a hundred yards, Jennings had a sudden thought. 'I say Darbi, you'd better let me have Matron's present. You don't look safe wobbling about like that with valuable cut-glass vases in your pocket.'

'You should have thought of that before,' grunted Darbishire through clenched teeth. 'I can't get it out of my pocket, now we've started.'

'Yes, you can. Steer with one hand, and I'll ride alongside while you get it and pass it over.'

Steer with one hand! A rash suggestion if ever there was one; and quite out of the question, considering that he needed both hands very firmly on the handlebars in order to stay on the machine at all! For by now he had reached the top of the hill, and the bicycle was freewheeling down the slope in the most alarming fashion.

Darbishire swallowed hard: he was going too fast – much too fast! He tugged on both brakes... Nothing happened!... The wheels spun round faster and faster, while the broken brake block clicked and rattled against the spokes like a fast-moving turnstile.

'Hi, Darbi! No need to go flat out. Slow down!' he heard Jennings call, from some distance behind him.

'It's no good... I can't stop!' Darbishire shouted back.

It was fortunate that there was no other traffic on the road, for by this time the machine was hurtling downhill at a brisk twenty miles an hour, while Darbishire bounced on the crossbar, and hoping for the best.

And then it happened! As he neared the bottom of the slope, his front wheel hit a stone lying in the roadway. The back wheel jerked up into the air, and the rider shot over the handlebars to make a sudden forced landing in the ditch.

Fortunately Darbishire's fall was cushioned by the soft damp earth, and, after the first gasp of surprise, he sat up and heaved a sigh of relief. He felt safer in the ditch than he had felt on the bicycle; and the abrupt ending to his ride had solved the problem of how he was ever going to dismount.

Shortly afterwards, Jennings freewheeled along to the scene of the accident.

'It's all right, Jen; no harm done,' Darbishire assured him, waving his arms to prove that no bones were broken. 'Everything's perfectly all right...'

He broke off suddenly as a tinkle of glass sounded from inside his raincoat pocket. His hand flew to his mouth in guilty realisation. Goodness! He had forgotten all about that!

Slowly he turned his pocket inside out and gaped in dismay at the fragments of the cut-glass vase which fell at his feet.

Jennings was furious. 'You clumsy hippo-potamus, Darbishire! Now what are we going to do? We can't give Matron a handful of ground glass.'

'Sorry,' Darbishire mumbled. 'But it wasn't my fault: my black brake brock – I mean my brock blake back...'

'Of *course* it was your fault! You needn't have gone vooming down the hill as though you were trying to burst through the supersonic barrier.'

'I didn't mean to. I couldn't help it if my back...'

'Oh, shut up about you back brake block being bloken. That's not going to help mend Matron's present.'

'All right; you needn't go on and *on* about it. Perhaps we can think of something else for her,' Darbishire answered. He righted his machine and trudged on towards the village in gloomy silence.

6

The Present for Matron

Jennings and Darbishire were not the only people for whom the afternoon was crowded with anxious moments. Mr Wilkins, too, was worried. For some time after lunch, he had paced the building deep in thought, and finally he had gone to consult Mr Carter about the problem preying on his mind.

He found his colleague marking books in the staff room.

'Look here, Carter, I want your advice on rather a confidential matter,' he began, in tones which were audible on the far side of the quad.

Mr Carter got up and closed the window. 'Yes, Wilkins; what can I do for you?'

'Well, I was a bit curt with Matron the other day. I jumped to the conclusion that a boy was pretending to be ill to avoid being kept in, and I told her she'd no right to send him to bed.'

Mr Wilkins had been feeling disturbed by the little misunderstanding ever since he had discovered himself to be in the wrong. He had made inquiries later on that day, and had found to his surprise that Jennings really *had* been suffering from a bilious attack. Mr Wilkins was sorry then that he had been so forthright in condemning Matron. He felt he should do something to remedy his rash criticism. Perhaps she was feeling offended... Perhaps an apology was called for... What did Mr Carter think?

'I should admit that you made a mistake,' Mr Carter advised. 'If you think you offended her, it would certainly be a good plan to extend the olive branch of peace, and...'

'Olive branch! Yes, good idea!' Mr Wilkins seized on the metaphor in a flash. 'I'll give her a bunch of flowers as a peace offering... She'll like that... Now, where can I get some flowers?'

He hurried out of the staff room and headed for the school gardens, pleased beyond measure at this happy solution to his problem.

But the gardens proved disappointing. Few flowers raised their heads on that chilly January afternoon, and Mr Wilkins soon had to revise his plan for gathering armfuls of luxuriant blooms. His eye ranged round the gardens without enthusiasm; leeks to his left, sprouts to his right. Whichever way he looked, he could find nothing suitable for a buttonhole – let alone a bouquet.

He walked on until he came to the small

garden plots which were tended by the boys. Here again there seemed to be nothing growing. Then, just as he was about to admit defeat, he caught sight of a clump of snowdrops in a sheltered spot near the wall.

Snowdrops... The very thing... Strictly speaking, of course, they were the property of one of the boys, but Mr Wilkins knew from experience how eager the boys always were for a bunch of their home-grown flowers to be accepted by some member of the staff. There would be time enough later on for him to find the owner of the plot, explain what he had done, and accept the boy's grateful thanks for being honoured in this way. So he picked all the snowdrops he could find, and hurried indoors to Matron's sitting-room.

There was no answer to his knock, so he left the flowers on a table just inside the door. He would return later and make his little speech of apology At the moment, however, he had other duties to attend to, for it was striking four o'clock and time to check that the boys had returned from their expeditions to the village.

The last two boys to return were Jennings and Darbishire. They arrived panting and breathless, just as the duty master was closing the register.

'We're back, sir. We're not late, are we, sir?' gasped Jennings.

'You certainly aren't *early*. Another two seconds and you would have lost your village leave for the rest of the term,' simmered Mr Wilkins.

Outside in the corridor, Darbishire said: 'Phew, talk about a narrow escape! I never thought we'd make it. I'm just about whacked after pelting full tilt from the village.'

'Huh, all very well for you to start moaning,' Jennings complained. 'It was you who bished things up in the first place. All that money spent – and nothing to give Matron, except a handful of ground glass!'

'Well, you did *mean* to give her something,' said Darbishire. 'My father says it's not the cost of a present that matters – it's the thought that you put behind it. It'd do just as well if you gave her something that didn't cost you anything at all.'

'Such as what? You know wizard well I haven't got anything she'd want. I could go on *thinking* about it till I was black in the face, but...' Jennings paused, as a brilliant idea flashed into his mind, 'I've got it, Darbi – flowers! I'll give her those snowdrops in my garden.'

'Coo, yes, wacko! And you can put plenty of thought behind them to make up for not giving her a cut-glass bowl to put them in. Let's go and pick them now.'

At full speed they raced out of the building

and headed for their garden plots. Jennings pulled up short when he reached his own small patch, and blinked at the empty flower bed in dismay.

'Oh, fish-hooks, they've all gone!' he exclaimed. 'Whatever's happened?'

For some moments they stood puzzling over the mystery.

'You must have picked them,' Darbishire decided.

'No, I haven't – honestly I've never even touched them.'

'Well, perhaps you picked them without knowing it. My father says that some people are often so absent-minded that...'

'Oh, don't be a coot, Darbishire! You don't think I'd go wandering round the gardens, gathering massive great bunches of foliage, without knowing what I was doing. There's been some supersonic sabotage some-where!... The whole thing's jolly sinister.'

Jennings led the way back indoors. 'It just shows that things are against us this afternoon,' he remarked. 'It's one of those mouldy days when everything decides to pick on us to happen to.'

Darbishire nodded in agreement. The memory of his cycling expedition was still vivid. 'I think you ought to go and tell Matron about her present, all the same,' he suggested.

'Present!... Which present?'

'The one you meant to give her. You've been to a lot of trouble over it, and you don't want to waste all the thought you've put behind it, do you?'

There was a grain of sense in what Darbishire said, so they went upstairs and tapped on the door of Matron's sitting-room. There was no answer: Jennings opened the door and looked inside.

At once, a cry of recognition burst from his lips.

'Gosh, look, Darbi! There are my snowdrops; *slap-bang-wallop* on the table just inside the door. How on earth do you think they got there?'

'Well, I expect what happened was that you...'

'Oh, shut up, Darbishire! It's bad enough being told I picked them without knowing it. Now, I suppose, you're going to make out I carried them up here in my sleep.'

'It doesn't really matter how they got here,' Darbishire pointed out. 'You ought to be pleased, really. Somebody's very decently saved you the fag of carting them all the way upstairs.' Jennings walked into the room and picked up the flowers. He was just arranging them tidily when Matron's light footstep was heard approaching along the corridor.

'She's coming!' hissed Darbishire, in a whisper, hoarse with suspense.

Flowers in hand, Jennings emerged from

the sitting-room and met Matron on the threshold. He thrust the bunch towards her.

'They're out of my garden, Matron. They're for you,' he mumbled. 'It's a little present because you've been so decent.'

She took the bunch from him. 'Thank you very much, Jennings. They're lovely!'

'They're not much really Matron. But I put a lot of thought behind them – five shillings' worth, as a matter of fact, and Darbishire helped too.'

Darbishire was hopping about in the doorway anxious not to miss his share of Matron's gratitude. 'Come along in, Darbishire,' she said. And then she caught sight of his socks, smeared from knee to ankle with oil from the chain of his hired bicycle. 'Good heavens! Surely you didn't get as dirty as that just picking flowers!'

'No, Matron,' he confessed. 'That's just my contribution to the thought behind your present.' He moved over and stood behind the table where his socks would be less noticeable.

Just then, a heavier footstep sounded in the corridor and Mr Wilkins appeared in the doorway. He glanced round the room noting the flowers in Matron's hand... Ah! So she had already found his little gift. He was about to embark on his speech of explanation when she said: 'Look at this lovely bunch of flowers, Mr Wilkins. Jennings has just given them to me.'

The room swam before Mr Wilkins' eyes: he clutched at the doorknob for support.

'I... I... Did you say *Jennings* had given you those flowers?'

'Yes; wasn't it kind of him!'

'But surely – you've made a mistake. Those flowers aren't from him.'

'Oh yes, they are, sir,' Jennings chimed in. 'They're out of my garden. Mine's the only plot that's got any snowdrops, sir.'

'Oh... I see.' Light dawned in Mr Wilkins' mind. So Jennings was the gardener in question – he *would* be! Too late, now, to seek his permission; and useless to pretend that the flowers were a peace offering. Disappointed, Mr Wilkins mumbled something about being on duty and made for the door.

'Must you go, Mr Wilkins?' asked Matron. 'You haven't told me yet what you came to see me about.'

'Oh ... er ... nothing, really. I just looked in to ... er, well...' He searched his mind for a suitable reason for his visit, and suddenly remembered a matter that he had been meaning to broach for some time. 'Ah, yes... Do you happen to know if any of the maids found a gold cufflink when they cleaned my room the other day?'

'I don't think so,' Matron answered. 'They'd have told me if they had. Have you lost one?'

'Yes. Can't think where the thing's got to. I thought I left them both on my dressing table and now I can only find one.'

For the last few days, Mr Wilkins had been feeling depressed by his loss. The cufflinks had been a twenty-first birthday present which his sister Margaret had given him many years before. Quite apart from their sentimental value, it was annoying to have to secure his shirt cuff with a paper-clip until such time as he could go into Dunhambury and buy himself another pair.

Jennings looked interested. 'Was it a square gold one with your initials on, sir?' he asked.

'That's right. Have you seen it anywhere?'

'Oh, yes; rather, sir.'

Mr Wilkins lost his worried look. 'Splendid; where is it?'

'Oh, I don't know where it is *now*, sir,' said Jennings; 'but if it's one of the pair you were wearing last week, I'll know what to look for. I'll make a note in my diary to remind me not to forget to keep my eyes open.'

'My father lost a pair of cufflinks at home once, sir,' Darbishire volunteered from behind the table. 'We had to take the floorboards up to find them. Would you like me to...?'

'No I would *not*, Darbishire,' said Mr Wilkins warmly. 'You're not taking any floorboards up in my room.'

'My father spotted them in the end though, sir. He's got eyes like a lynx...' He broke off, delighted by what seemed to him to be a brilliant pun. 'Oh, I say did you hear that? I almost made a supersonic joke, quite by accident. I said, my father...'

'We heard,' said Mr Wilkins curtly.

Matron was wondering where to put the flowers. The only vessels available were two tall vases on the mantelpiece, neither of which were suitable for the short-stalked snowdrops. 'What a pity I haven't got anything the right size,' she said. 'What I really want is a cut-glass bowl.'

Darbishire looked away unable to meet the reproach in Jennings' eyes. But to Mr Wilkins the words came as an inspiration.

'A cut-glass bowl; why I've got the very thing in my room! I bought it last term and I've never used it. I shall be only too pleased, Matron, if you will accept it as a little present.'

Without waiting for a reply he hurried away and returned a few moments later with an exact replica of Jennings' ill-fated gift. 'There we are, Matron – what about that?' he exclaimed heartily.

'That's very kind of you, Mr Wilkins,' she said, as she took the gift. 'I am lucky today; first Jennings gives me flowers, and now you give me a cut-glass bowl.'

'Funny thing that,' mused Mr Wilkins. 'I

had intended to give you a bunch of flowers.'

'And I *was* going to give you a cut-glass bowl,' added Jennings.

'Really! I wonder why you both changed your minds!'

'Well – I – er–' said Jennings, and immediately became tongue-tied.

'The fact is, Matron–' said Mr Wilkins, and then relapsed into silence.

The two donors looked at each other with a new interest. For the first time in five terms, Jennings and Mr Wilkins found themselves working together in a common cause.

It was a new experience for both of them.

Unfortunately Jennings and Mr Wilkins proved to be uneasy allies and the bond between them was soon broken.

The trouble started in class the following day. Jennings was never at his best during Mr Wilkins' geometry lessons, and on that particular Thursday afternoon he was soon at a loss to understand the maze of angles, triangles and quadrilaterals which the master was drawing so freely all over the blackboard. It was a complicated diagram which put Jennings in mind of the sort of puzzle which requires the solver to find his way to the buried treasure in the middle of a maze, without becoming lost down blind turnings.

Mr Wilkins, however, seemed to be enjoying his quest for treasure. He strode up and down the classroom, talking enthusiastically of parallelograms, and full of praise for lines bisected by a point.

Jennings' mind wandered from Mr Wilkins' argument to Mr Wilkins' cufflink, and he remembered that he had promised to make a note of the tragic loss in his diary... Oh yes, and while he was about it he would enter the details of the debt which Venables had incurred by borrowing a lollipop during break that morning.

With a watchful eye on Mr Wilkins, Jennings took the diary from his pocket, turned to the memoranda page and jotted down a few notes in his secret code. Then, quite naturally his mind veered off on another tack, and he was no longer a small boy in the back row of a geometry class, but a secret service agent tapping out messages in code on a portable wireless transmitter... *Have kidnapped the enemy's Chief of Staff ... stop... Please send fast plane...*

'Jennings!' Mr Wilkins' vast voice ripped through the boy's wool-gathering wits and brought him back to reality with a start.

'Er – yes, sir?'

'Have you copied down that figure from the blackboard yet?'

'No, sir; I didn't know we had to.'

'You didn't know...! But you were writing

something down a few moments ago – I saw you.'

Jennings glanced down at his desk: the ink was still wet on the memoranda page of his diary. 'That was ... that was nothing much, sir.'

Mr Wilkins bristled dangerously. 'Do you mean to tell me that you were writing something in my lesson that wasn't what I'd set? Read it out at once.'

Jennings gulped. 'I can't, sir. I don't think I can pronounce it.'

'Do as I tell you, and don't make trumpery excuses.'

Pens went down all round the room as Form 3 sat up and prepared to follow the proceedings with a lively interest.

Haltingly Jennings read aloud: *'Selbanev sewo em eno popillol.'*

Mr Wilkins looked blank. 'I beg your pardon?' he inquired.

'It's in code, sir. You see, I was making a note in my diary.'

An angry *Corwumph!* shattered the still calm of the classroom as Mr Wilkins gave vent to his feelings. 'Writing your diary in class... Never heard of such a thing! Bring it up to me, at once.'

He went on *corwumph*-ing softly to himself until the diary was placed on the desk before him. Then he focused his gaze on the memoranda pages, his eyes popping in bewilderment. 'What on earth does all this nonsense mean?' he demanded.

'It isn't nonsense, sir – it's my code. You have to write the words backwards,' Jennings explained. Warming to his task, he translated: 'This sentence means – er – "Venables owes me one lollipop," sir.'

'Oh, I don't, sir! I paid it back after lunch,' Venables protested warmly.

'Be quiet, Venables,' barked Mr Wilkins. 'I never heard such a lot of trumpery moonshine in my life... All this ridiculous *Selbanev popillol* nonsense!'

'Oh but, sir, I *did* pay it back! Jennings has forgotten to cross it off,' insisted the lollipop borrower.

'I... I... Corwumph! Will you be quiet, *Selbanev* – er – I mean, Venables!' Mr Wilkins rounded sharply upon the interrupter. 'We are in the middle of an important geometry lesson. This is no time to start worrying about your miserable *popillols* – er – *pollypips*...'

'Lollipops, sir.'

'That's what I said – more or less.' Mr Wilkins turned his attention again to the diary, and a frown of annoyance clouded his brow as he pored over the next entry.

Retsim Snikliw – gnissim knil, it said. 'Very interesting, I'm sure. Unfortunately for you, Jennings, I can work this out for myself.' And with an accuracy that would have done credit to an experienced solver of ciphers, he announced in ringing tones: 'Mister Wilkins – missing link!'

There was a burst of laughter from the class.

'Yes, that's right, sir,' Jennings agreed. 'I just thought I'd make a note, so I shouldn't forget.'

It was an unfortunate misunderstanding. For to Mr Wilkins, whose thoughts were far removed from shirt cuffs, the phrase 'missing link' conjured up a picture of a sub-human anthropoid monster, swinging among the treetops in some dark, prehistoric era.

'I... I... How dare you say I'm the missing link!' he spluttered.

'But I didn't, sir. I meant...'

'Don't try to deny it, boy! Here it is in black and white in your diary; and what's more, you've written it in some ridiculous code and tried to make a secret of it... Well, I won't *have* it kept a secret. I – I mean–' Mr Wilkins' words trailed away in speechless indignation.

'Oh, but there's no secret about it, sir,' Jennings assured him. 'Lots of people know you've got a link missing. I don't think you quite understand, sir.'

'I understand perfectly well, Jennings,' Mr Wilkins said when his powers of speech had returned. 'I shall confiscate this diary until the end of term, and report the facts to the headmaster.'

Confiscate the diary!... Jennings was aghast: a chill, empty feeling crept over him... Why if his diary was taken away he would be unable to keep his good resolution – let alone claim ten shillings from Aunt Angela at the end of the year!

He'd been proud of his record, too. Nearly a whole month had passed, and he hadn't missed recording a single day. And now this had to happen! The whole business seemed to him grossly unfair; after all, he'd only been trying to help by making a note about the lost cufflink. Admittedly, he had chosen the wrong time to do it, but why should Mr Wilkins regard the matter as a personal insult...?

'Please sir, couldn't I have some other punishment?' Jennings pleaded. 'You see, I promised my aunt to write something in my diary every day, and she'll be terribly upset if I don't, sir.'

Aunt Angela's grievous disappointment was wasted on Mr Wilkins. 'You shouldn't make these rash promises,' he said unfeelingly. 'Now go back to your place, and copy down that figure from the board.'

7

Assorted Fossils

For a fortnight, Jennings wrote his diary in a spare exercise book. He kept the entries short, as he planned to copy them all into his diary when at last it was returned to him. Even so, he soon began to despair of the task which lay ahead, because so much happened during the next fortnight that very soon he had filled up a dozen pages reporting the events of the day.

For it was during this time that the Form 3 museum was founded. The enterprise started off in an atmosphere of unbounded optimism, as a result of an astonishing discovery made by Darbishire.

He was digging his patch of garden during break one morning, when he unearthed an object which he felt sure was the fang of a prehistoric monster. He called to Jennings who was weeding in an adjoining plot.

'Wow! I say, look what I've found... A genuine hippogriff's tusk.'

'A genuine *what?*' queried Jennings, looking with interest at the mouldering piece of bone that his friend was waving in the air.

'Well, it's either the tusk of a hippogriff, or some animal jolly like it.'

'But there *is* no animal like it,' Jennings pointed out.

'Not now, of course – that's what makes it so rare. Funny to think it's been lying in my vegetable patch since the Bronze Age.'

They examined the 'find' carefully. When the mud had been wiped off with Darbishire's handkerchief, they found that the relic consisted of a four-inch length of discoloured ivory. At one end was a hole, which suggested that the original owner had been in the habit of sharpening his teeth on the Bronze Age rocks.

Jennings' recent visit to the Natural History Museum entitled him to speak as an expert on prehistoric animals; and, after a few moments of frowning thought, he gave his opinion. The tusk had clearly belonged to some extinct monster, he decided: probably not a genuine hippogriff, as that species had never existed, except in legend. On the other hand, it might well have belonged to a *bogus* hippogriff. There was no doubt, he maintained, that the fang was well fossilised, slightly ossified and possibly a little petrified as well.

Darbishire listened to the scientific discourse with close attention.

'Jolly good!' he said. 'You know, Jen, we could start quite a decent museum if we could find any more of these petrified specimens lying about.' His eyes lit up with enthusiasm as the possibilities of the scheme ran through his mind. 'We could have a natural history department with tadpoles and rare coots' eggs and things, and an ordinary history department with say for instance, bits of stone from the Stone Age and chunks of old iron from the Iron Age.'

The news of the venture spread, and very soon the rest of Form 3 had volunteered to keep their eyes open for any prehistoric remains and valuable museum pieces which might be lying about the school grounds. By the end of the week, the exhibits were being handed in faster than the curators could cope with them: already Jennings' desk was so crammed with objects of doubtful value that he was unable to close the lid.

'It's no good, Darbishire; we'll jolly well have to find a decent place where we can spread all the stuff out and label it,' Jennings said, as they were changing after football on Saturday afternoon. 'I vote we ask if we can use the hobbies room.'

'Sound scheme,' Darbishire agreed. 'And we must get everything properly labelled in Latin, just as they do in the British Museum. I'll take on that job, if you like.'

Mr Carter was on duty in the changing-room. He welcomed the idea of a small-scale museum, but he was not keen on having the well-equipped hobbies room used as a storehouse for the contents of the school waste-paper baskets. Instead, he suggested that they might use an empty attic on the top floor for this temple of culture which they had in mind.

'Thanks very much, sir,' said Jennings eagerly. 'That'll be just the place for our rare relics and ancient antiques. Come on, Darbi, let's go and get things organised, right away.'

They dashed out of the changing-room and up the stairs. On the first landing, they met Venables and Atkinson.

'Supersonic news! Mr Carter's given us permish to use the top floor,' Jennings informed them. 'That means we'll have masses of room; so if you characters want a job, you can scout round and see if you can find any more priceless junk and stuff.'

'Wacko! Let's go and scrounge round the tuck-box room, Atki – there should be something decent there.' The volunteers turned and hurried away on their scavenging mission.

Mr Wilkins was emerging from the staff room, and Jennings decided that this would be a good moment to secure his co-operation.

'Sir, Mr Wilkins, sir! We're searching for ancient relics, sir,' he began. 'Do you think we might have a quick look in the staff room to see if there are any old fossils lying about?'

Unfortunately, Mr Wilkins jumped to the wrong conclusion. He turned three shades pinker.

'Old fossils in the staff room! I... I... Are you trying to be funny, boy?'

'No, sir, honestly I mean things for my museum. You know, like stuffed birds and that sort of stuff, sir.'

'Well, you won't find anything stuffed in the staff room – except the cushions,' Mr Wilkins replied. 'And I'll tell you another thing, Jennings; when *I'm* on duty I don't intend to have the building cluttered knee-deep in rubbish.'

'Oh, no; we'll be ever so careful, sir.'

They spent the next half-hour removing the exhibits from Jennings' desk and arranging them in the attic. It was an excellent room for their purpose, for along one wall ran a broad shelf on which they mounted their display. Pride of place was reserved for the prehistoric tusk; on its left were ranged marine objects such as shells, dried seaweed and old bottles found on the beach. The bottles, though empty, were of particular interest for they *might*, at some time, have borne messages from mariners in distress. Then there was the box of smooth round stones – displayed on the right – any of which might have contained a fossil.

'But how do we know they've got fossils inside, unless we break them open?' Jennings queried. 'After all, it was mostly feeble characters like Binns minor and Blotwell who collected them, and I bet none of that mob can tell just from the outside.'

'Binns says he can tell by instinct,' Darbishire explained. 'He looks at a stone very hard, and he gets a restless sort of feeling if there's a fossil in it. Of course, it's not very scientific, but it's easier than cracking them open.'

In order to be on the safe side, the *Binns-Blotwell Collection* was labelled: *Smooth round stones – probably fossilised, but possibly not.*

'I can't put all that into Latin,' Darbishire complained. 'I've only got a small vocab. at the back of my grammar book, and it's not much good, except for things like *The queen's tables*, and *The spears of the slave*.'

'What about ossified hippogriff's tusk? Does it give that?'

Darbishire thumbed his way through the vocabulary 'No good at all,' he said. 'I shall have to call it, *Monstrous tooth of an animal*. I can just about translate that, if you're not fussy about genitive singulars, and things.'

Atkinson arrived just then. His search behind the pipes in the tuck-box room had yielded nothing of value, but he had had the good fortune to find a shrivelled starfish behind the bootlockers.

'What about this then? I've got something pretty rare here – an extinct starfish,' he announced,

'Starfishes aren't extinct,' Jennings pointed out.

'*This* one is. It became extinct one day last summer when the tide went out.'

Atkinson looked round the exhibits with interest; and, when his eyes lighted on the *monstrous tooth,* he said: 'I see you've resurrected the old knife handle I chucked away the term before last.'

The curators felt a sudden concern. 'Knife handle! Don't he such an ignorant bazooka,' said Jennings. 'It's a petrified fang. Darbishire found it in his garden.'

'I'm not surprised – that's where I chucked it. It's an old thing I used to keep in my tuck-box for cutting chunks of cake.'

'I bet you what you like you're wrong! Why any one can see it's as ancient as a school bun.'

Jennings thrust the relic under Atkinson's nose. 'Look, you can even see where the monster's worn a hole in it, sharpening it on the rocks.'

'You must be stark, raving cuckoo,' said Atkinson. 'That's the hole where the blade part fitted in.'

The curators looked more closely – and were forced to admit that there might be some truth in Atkinson's story.

'H'm... I think you'd better alter the label, Darbi,' Jennings decided.

'I can't... I don't know the Latin for "monstrous knife handle".'

'Well, it doesn't matter, anyway,' said Jennings. 'We've got plenty of other things to be going on with, that really *are* genuine.'

The work of collecting and arranging occupied most of the boys' free time during the next few days. Temple and Bromwich major undertook to supply the natural history section with plaster casts of animal footprints. They obtained excellent impressions of a cart horse's hoof and a seagull's foot, but they were less successful with a cast of the hind paw of Matron's cat, whose impression they found on the quad... For Mr Wilkins, hurrying across to investigate what they were doing, accidentally walked across the plaster before it was dry. In this way they acquired a cast that showed a cat's paw-mark on one side, and Mr Wilkins' left heel on the other. After some argument they threw it away, as they decided that Mr Wilkins might object when he found his footprints classified amongst the natural history exhibits.

As the collection grew, so Jennings became more particular about accepting articles of doubtful value. He was quite indignant when Venables arrived on one of his frequent visits to the attic, bearing a distemper brush which he had found in the potting shed.

'I thought you might like this, because the bristles are genuine badger hair,' Venables explained. 'So if anyone wants to know what sort of hair a genuine badger's got he can...'

'Oh, don't be such a clodpoll,' Jennings broke in. 'That sort of thing's no earthly use. If it comes to that, I've got a camel hair brush in my paintbox. Might as well put that on the shelf, in case anyone wants to see what sort of hairbrush a genuine camel uses!'

'That's not the same thing at all,' Venables argued. 'Still, if you don't like that – what about *this?*' He produced two sticks of wood from his pocket and held them out for the curator's inspection.

'What are they?' demanded Jennings suspiciously.

'Native method of lighting fires,' announced Venables proudly. 'Africans in the jungle rub them together, and after a bit they get hot and start smoking.'

Jennings looked interested. 'Yes, I suppose they *would* find it warm work.'

Venables tapped his forehead sadly. 'You're bats! I don't mean the *natives* start smoking – I mean the sticks do. Then they light the fire. It's true – honestly. Mr Carter told us about it in geography.'

'Oh, well; if *he* says it's genuine, I suppose

it must be.' Jennings took the sticks and examined them. 'How does Mr Carter know these came from Africa?... They look like ordinary bits of firewood to me.'

'Well, as a matter of fact, that's what they are,' Venables admitted reluctantly.

'But you just told me they came from the African jungle.'

'Oh no, I didn't. I said the natives used pieces of wood *like* these. Any bits of wood will do really, so I thought if chaps wanted to know how to light fires in the jungle...'

Venables broke off and dodged smartly as Jennings hurled the sticks of firewood at him.

'Buzz off, Venables! If you can't find anything better to do than to come here wasting our time with old paint brushes and sticks of firewood...! This is a serious museum, I'd have you know, and we don't want it cluttered up with junk.'

A few days later, Mr Carter came upstairs to see what progress was being made. He was not impressed with the shrivelled starfish, the empty bottles and the possibly fossilised stones.

'Surely you can find something more interesting than these?' he said. 'You've nothing here that's worth looking at.'

The curators' disappointment showed on their faces. They knew in their hearts that the criticism was justified... On the other hand, was it *their* fault that the school grounds were so lacking in valuable relics?

'What other sort of museumy things could we have then, sir?' Jennings asked. 'There doesn't seem to be any genuine ossified ruins anywhere around these parts, sir.'

Mr Carter considered. The district around Linbury was particularly rich in historical associations. There was, for example, the site of the old Roman encampment on the Downs, close by the Dunhambury road. The place was well worth a visit, even though the remains of the Roman occupation had long since been removed to the Dunhambury museum.

The two boys were delighted when Mr Carter suggested this.

'Supersonic idea, sir!' Jennings hopped excitedly from foot to foot. 'We could go there on Sunday couldn't we, Darbi?'

'Mind you, you're not likely to find anything there *now*,' Mr Carter warned them. 'The experts made a very thorough search, you know.'

'Yes, but there'd be no harm in just *looking*, would there, sir?' Jennings persisted. Here was an excuse for an expedition, and he was not going to be put off by any thoughts of failure.

Mr Carter was impressed with their enthusiasm. 'As a matter of fact, I've been meaning, for some time, to take a party of boys to Dunhambury to see the remains in the museum there,' he told them. 'Now that you seem keen on forming a collection of your own, I'll see what I can do about it.'

That evening, Jennings made an appeal to Mr Wilkins for the return of his diary. Already the exercise book he was using as a stop-gap was half full, and the task of copying the entries back into the little red diary would be unending if it were not tackled soon... He hurried along to Mr Wilkins' room, and knocked at the door.

'Sir, please sir: do you think you could possibly let me have my diary back, please? It's terribly important, sir.'

Mr Wilkins refused to see the urgency of the situation. 'Of course you can't have it back. I told you I'd confiscated it for the remainder of the term.'

Jennings changed his line of approach. 'Well, sir, would you very kindly agree to *lend* it to me just for a few days so I can keep it up to date. Then I'll give it back to you, sir.'

'*Lend* it to you!... Sounds a queer way of dealing with confiscated property,' said Mr Wilkins. 'I might as well be running a public library, if you're going to pop in here every few days to borrow a book.'

He pondered over the request for a few moments and at last decided that it was a reasonable one... Keeping diaries was, after all, a thing to be encouraged.

He fetched the little red book from his cupboard and handed it to the grateful owner.

'Here you are, then; but it's only on loan, mind. I'll give you till Monday evening to copy it up to date, and then I'll have it back.' Mr Wilkins was quite firm on this point. *He'd* show these boys that he was not the sort of man whose threats were idle!

'Yes, sir; willingly, sir.'

Jennings hurried away with the precious book. It was too late to start copying the entries that night, for the dormitory bell was already sounding.

He *meant* to make a start during break the next morning, but no sooner had he spread out the exercise book and opened his diary than Darbishire arrived bearing the prongs of a small garden fork which he had found in the tool shed.

'How about this for excavating the remains with on Sunday?' he asked, waving the implement round his head and making little jabs at the air. 'It's got the handle missing, but it digs quite well. I've just been trying it out on a corner of the football pitch.'

Jennings shook his head. 'You seem to forget that Mr Carter said there was nothing there to dig. It's all been taken away by the

107

archi – er – what-do-you-call-them?'

'Archipelagos?'

'No – archaeologists – the old boys who did the digging.'

'Huh! I bet they missed a few things,' said Darbishire knowingly 'Those experts are all the same... Short-sighted professors and fossilised old geezers – probably so absentminded that they've forgotten to take half the stuff away! My father knew an old archi – er – one of these digging characters once and...'

'I dare say, but we haven't got time for his life story now,' Jennings said curtly. 'It's Friday already, and if we're going on a highly organised scientific digging expedition the day after tomorrow, we'd better start thinking about it.'

He flipped over the leaves of his diary until he came to a convenient page for making notes. 'We'll just draw up a list of equipment and raw materials and things first,' he said.

'Well, we've got a fork to dig with,' Darbishire pointed out, 'and we shan't need any other equipment, except our raincoats.'

Jennings *tut-tutted* in kindly despair.

'You've got no more idea of organising a scientific expedition, Darbi, than – than this ink-pot.' And he waved the ink-pot in his friend's face to prove the point. 'Now, first of all, we must make a list of all the things we'll need.'

'Such as what?'

'Well, we'll have to have some provisions for a kick-off. All decent expeditions take rations. We shall be there at least half an hour, don't forget; and you need to keep your strength up while you're digging.'

'Food – yes, of course!' Darbishire's eyes sparkled... This was even better than he'd hoped for! 'I've got a box of liquorice allsorts and a bunch of bananas in my tuck-box,' he volunteered.

'That'll do; and we shall need a bag to put the remains in.'

'There won't *be* any remains! We could eat that lot, easily.'

'No, you clodpoll. The *Roman* remains we're going to dig up,' Jennings explained impatiently. He rested the diary on his knee and wrote: *List of Materials Required for Expedition to the Roman Camp.*

'I should have said, *Ad castram romanum,*' suggested Darbishire.

Jennings paused in the act of underlining his entry. 'Where on earth's that?'

'It's the same place, in Latin,' Darbishire explained. 'After all, the Romans didn't speak English, and my father says...'

'Oh, shut up, Darbishire. How can I concentrate on scientific equipment with you nattering down my ear?'

He bent once more to his task. Underneath the heading, he wrote:

Item No. 1 – Liquorice allsorts - Bag of
Item No. 2 – Bananas - Bunch of
Item No. 3 – Garden fork - Part of
Item No. 4 –

The expedition was beginning to take shape.

8

The Rattling Relic

At the far end of the school grounds, where the playing fields give place to farmland, a narrow pathway leads across the meadow and winds its way up the landward slope of the South Downs. The track skirts the village of Linbury and comes out on the Dunhambury road not far from the old Roman campsite.

Jennings and Darbishire made use of this short cut when they started off on their expedition the following Sunday afternoon. They had made their plans with care, and their pockets bulged with provisions, small tools and paper bags for the collection and storage of Roman remains.

Jennings had brought his diary in order to make a list of their finds, and Darbishire carried a Latin vocabulary, so that he could translate them into their original language.

'H'm, there's not much to see, is there?' Jennings observed, when they arrived at the bare expanse of downland.

A bronze memorial tablet on a stone pillar informed the public of the discoveries which

111

had been made in the vicinity; but apart from this there was nothing to show that the area had once echoed to the sound of Roman voices and throbbed to the tread of Roman feet.

'This is the spot right enough,' said Darbishire, slipping out of his raincoat. 'You want to use your imagination, Jen, and try to see the place as it used to be round about Nero's time... I can just picture the old Roman soldiers putting up their tents and cooking their baked beans in their billy-cans, and enjoying a good old camp fire sing-song by the light of their Roman candles.'

'Gosh, yes! That would have been worth listening to, wouldn't it?' said Jennings, conjuring up the scene in his mind's eye. He stepped up on to a molehill and announced: 'Ladies and Gentlemen! For our next item, Julius Caesar will sing "John Brown's Body."'

Darbishire was shocked by this display of ignorance. 'You mean John Brown's *Corpus*. He wouldn't have sung in English, you know; the whole programme would have been in Latin.' He took his vocabulary from his pocket and tried to find the Latin for 'campfire sing-song.' He was disappointed. 'They probably called it a *chantus-chantus*, or something like that,' he hazarded.

But Jennings had returned to the practical

112

problems of the Twentieth Century. 'We haven't come here for a *chantus-chantus*,' he pointed out curtly. 'We've come here to dig up remains, and the sooner we get down to it the better.'

For half an hour they crawled about on hands and knees, digging little holes at random in the ground. They found a broken milk bottle and the top of a fountain pen, but no relics of the Roman occupation came to light. So they moved farther afield and tried again near a clump of gorse bushes, some distance to their right – still without result.

Finally Jennings said: 'I reckon we've come to the wrong place, Darbi. I've dug halfway down to Australia already and I haven't seen a whisker of a prehistoric remain yet.'

'Well, Mr Carter did *say* those old archaeologist geezers had dug most of the things up. They've been trained, you see. It doesn't matter how long a thing's been lying in the earth, those chaps always find it. They know where to look for things, even though they were buried years before they were born.'

Jennings laid the garden fork on the turf beside him. 'You do say the most cootish things, Darbishire. How can anyone be buried before he was born?'

'No, I meant – well, you know what I

mean... Look, how would it be if we had a spot of provisions now: I'm so empty inside I'm beginning to rattle.'

They ate the bananas and the liquorice allsorts. Then, because Mr Carter was always reminding them not to leave litter about, Jennings began digging a hole in which they could bury the banana skins.

He had reached a depth of several inches before it occurred to him that they had already dug more than a score of holes – any of which would have suited their purpose equally well.

'We'd better start filling some of these holes in, Darbi,' he suggested. 'This place is beginning to look more like a rabbits' housing estate than a Roman camp.'

So Darbishire filled in while Jennings dug... And then, quite unexpectedly it happened!

Jennings jabbed the fork into the earth and felt the prongs hit against something hard and unyielding. He jabbed again in a different place, and once more the fork met with an obstruction. Excitedly he scooped away the loose earth with one hand, while he went on plying the fork with the other... There was no doubt about it – there was *something* there! Metal too, he judged, from the sound of it.

'Hey, Darbi. Come over here quickly I think I've found something!'

Darbishire came, but without much hope. He was fast losing faith in the enterprise.

'Listen, Darbi. The fork's just hit something hard,' Jennings exclaimed breathlessly. He jabbed the prongs down again, and this time he heard them strike. 'There it is again – a sort of metallic ring.'

Darbishire peered into the shallow hole. 'I can't see a metallic ring,' he said.

'Of course you can't *see* it. It's the sort of ring you *hear*...' Jennings scooped away more loose earth with his hands, and a moment later he was pointing triumphantly at a piece of rusty iron, just visible at the bottom of the hole.

'Gosh, you're right! There *is* something there,' Darbishire breathed. 'Looks like a metallic ring – the sort you *fasten* things to, I mean.'

Soon they had cleared away enough earth to see that their discovery was a link in what seemed to be a chain of some length. It was not buried very deeply and further exploration showed that it stretched lengthways for a yard or two, just below ground level. Things were easier then: as soon as the first two links were laid bare, the boys heaved with all their might and the chain broke through the surface.

'Wacko – it's coming!... Heave harder, Darbi.'

'I *am* heaving harder!... Isn't this exciting!

My father says you never know... Oh, gosh, what's happened?' He broke off puzzled. For by now, the last link had appeared above the level of the earth; yet although they heaved and strained with all their might, it refused to come clear of the ground.

They gazed at each other in hopeful wonder. Was there, perhaps, something on the end of the chain?...

There was!... But it took a further twenty minutes' hard digging to loosen the earth from it. Then, another lively tug of war ... and they saw that the object attached to the chain was a large, iron-tyred wheel. It was in a poor state of preservation, for some of the spokes were broken, the hub was rotten with age, and the rim was red with rust.

'Petrified paint-pots, what a find!' gasped Darbishire. 'And what a size! It's big enough for a tractor.'

'Don't be a coot! The Romans didn't have tractors – they had chariots. Don't just stand there with your eyes popping in and out like organ-stops. Help me clean it up a bit.'

But Darbishire could only stand and gape. 'You mean to tell me that this is a genuine, guaranteed, prehistoric, Roman chariot wheel!'

'Bound to be! Why else should it be on a genuine, guaranteed, prehistoric Roman

116

campsite,' Jennings returned logically. 'Besides, you can see by looking at it, if you know anything about Roman history.'

'I'm afraid I don't – much. Do you?'

Jennings frowned thoughtfully. 'Well, I'm not an expert, of course, but I know enough to recognise a chariot wheel when I see one. I'd say this was a pretty old specimen – *circa* fifty-five BC.'

Darbishire looked puzzled. '*Circa?*' he queried.

'Yes, that's Latin. It means *round*.'

'Well, of course it's round. You don't have to be a brain at Roman history to know they didn't have square wheels.'

'No, I meant the date – round about fifty-five BC. In Roman figures, of course, that'll be, er – LV BC.'

There was never any doubt in their minds about the next move. The wheel must be taken back to school to become the centre-piece of their museum. Later, perhaps, well-known archaeologists might be invited to come and inspect this interesting relic of classical craftsmanship: they might even write articles about it for learned magazines.

The boys heaved the wheel into an upright position. It was too heavy to carry, so they stood one on each side and rolled it along the path. At times the going was difficult for the wheel was liable to topple sideways or run over any incautious toe that happened to be in the way: before they had gone very far, they were beginning to wish that the Romans had made their chariot wheels from some lightweight alloy instead of wood and iron.

But it was the clanking chain trailing from the hub which caused them most trouble. Where the track was overgrown, the chain caught on every bush and tree stump in its path; and where the ground was firmer underfoot, the rattle of the chain and the rumble of the rim made as much noise as a steamroller on a cobblestoned road.

'We may have a bit of a job getting it upstairs to the attic,' Darbishire said, as they crashed their way up the gravel drive which led to the rear entrance of Linbury Court.

'Don't worry; we'll manage somehow,' Jennings replied. 'The shelf won't be strong enough to take the weight, so we'll move the whole collection on to the floor and put this *slap-bang* into the middle. It'll look a wizard sight better than Atkinson's defunct starfish.'

Mr Carter was halfway through the crossword puzzle in the Sunday paper when a knock sounded on his study door. It was a loud knock, rather as though someone were attacking the panels with a sledge hammer; and Mr Carter knew at once who had come to see him. Only one member of the staff

118

signalled his approach with such a volume of sound.

'Come in, Wilkins,' he called, laying down his paper with a sigh.

The door shivered on its hinges and Mr Wilkins strode in.

'Ah, I thought I'd find you in your study, Carter. You don't mind my popping in for a few minutes, do you?'

'No, no; not at all.'

Mr Carter gave up all thoughts of finishing his crossword puzzle. He knew that whenever Mr Wilkins chose to 'pop in' to anyone's room, all hope of a quiet afternoon usually 'popped out.' Today, however, looked like being the exception, for his colleague had come in search of rest and quiet. Wearily he sank into an armchair and put his feet on the fender.

'Ah, that's better,' Mr Wilkins exclaimed. 'Being on duty all day on Sunday is most exhausting. On the go all the time with hardly a moment to call your own.' He settled himself comfortably and closed his eyes.

He felt he could afford to relax now, for most of the boys had returned from their Sunday afternoon walks and were quietly reading books or writing. All being well, he could look forward to enjoying an hour's leisure, undisturbed by the demands of seventy-nine boys ... all being well!

Mr Carter took up his crossword puzzle again. It was quiet in the room, now that his colleague's eyes were glazing over in a well-earned doze. Drowsily Mr Wilkins murmured: 'You know, Carter, if there's one thing I enjoy when I get the chance, it's a quiet, peaceful Sunday afternoon.'

As his words died away a violent tumult shattered the stillness of the room. First came a resounding *jingle-jingle clank ... jingle-jingle clank*, as though a party of chain-rattling ghosts had combined to haunt some lonely manor house. Then, rumbling bumps and thuds beyond the door suggested that someone was trying to drive a Centurion tank up the stairs.

Mr Wilkins shot out of his chair like a fighter pilot on an ejector-seat.

'I... I... Cor-wumph!' he barked. 'What on earth's that ghastly commotion?'

'Nothing to get alarmed about,' said Mr Carter calmly. 'I expect it's only a couple of boys tiptoeing upstairs in their house-shoes. When you've been teaching as long as I have, Wilkins, you'll get used to the patter of little feet.'

'Yes – but, dash it all, Carter – I mean. Well, *listen* to it!'

The noise was growing even louder. It was as though the heavy thud of a pile-driver and the clatter of a bulldozer demolishing a Dutch barn had been added to the general hurly-burly.

'M'yes. It *does* sound rather disturbing. Perhaps you'd better go and investigate, as you're on duty,' Mr Carter suggested.

But Mr Wilkins was already heading for the door. 'I'll teach them to make that noise just when I'm trying to snatch a few minutes' rest,' he fumed. 'Just wait till I...' He hurled open the door and strode out on to the landing.

Jennings and Darbishire had struggled up fourteen stairs with their museum piece, bumping it up a step at a time on their journey to the top floor. Then, they had come to the awkward part where the narrow attic stairs turned a corner.

'She's biffing the wall on my side. Take her a bit more towards you,' Jennings had gasped.

'She won't go! She's hard up against the banisters already,' Darbishire had panted back.

'Well, we've got to get her round somehow, whether she'll go or not. You heave and I'll shove, and we'll see what happens.'

Mr Wilkins also saw what happened, for it was then that he emerged from Mr Carter's study to see the stairs blocked from side to side with a large wheel firmly wedged between the banisters. Trailing down the stairs was a rusty iron chain.

'I... I... What in the name of reason are you *silly* little boys playing at?' he demanded angrily. 'Take that gruesome collection of scrap metal off the stairs at once.'

Jennings was shocked by this lack of respect for a historical relic. 'Oh, but, sir, it's not scrap metal,' he protested. 'It's a Roman chariot wheel, sir.'

'Yes, sir, *circa* LV BC,' Darbishire added; and then, as Mr Wilkins continued to stare in blank amazement, he explained: 'That's the date, sir. I thought you'd like to know.'

Speech returned to Mr Wilkins. 'Have you gone off your head, Darbishire? What do you mean by standing there announcing the date as though you were a perpetual calendar. I know the date perfectly well. It's February the fourteenth, and that's no reason for turning the staircase into a blacksmith's shop. I will not have the building cluttered, waist-deep in rusty old iron. Take that rattling monstrosity outside and get rid of it... Bury it in the kitchen garden!'

Jennings thought it would be a pity to bury their treasured museum piece: after all, they had only just dug it up! He would like to have explained this to Mr Wilkins, but one look at the master's face warned him that this was not a good moment for explanations.

'Come on then, Darbi, let's have another bash.'

This time, Jennings heaved while Darbi-shire shoved – all to no purpose. The wheel's rim was stuck fast in the banisters, and the boys' efforts to dislodge it merely caused further havoc and confusion.

'Sorry sir, it won't budge,' Jennings was forced to admit.

Mr Wilkins almost danced with exasper-ation. 'You... you *silly* little boys... What did you want to *do* it for?' His voice rose to a squeak of annoyance. 'Here, mind out of the way both of you. I'll soon shift it.'

He strode up the stairs and rattled the priceless relic in an effort to work it loose. Chips of paint flew off the banisters and streaks of rust appeared on Mr Wilkins' best suit wherever the wheel's rim rubbed against it... 'Tut, tut, tut! It's so firmly wedged I ... can't ... move ... it ... at ... all,' panted Mr Wilkins, taking a fresh pull at each syllable.

A crowd of fascinated spectators had been forming at the foot of the stairs, ever since the first bumps and thuds had warned them that some interesting event was being organised for their enjoyment. Each recur-ring crash brought further groups hurrying to the scene and elbowing their way to the front, to make sure they missed no item in this entertaining programme.

Soon the audience was complete. Of the seventy-nine boarders of Linbury Court

School, seventy-seven were jamming the landing and overflowing on to the stairs. The remaining two were trying to keep out of Mr Wilkins' way and wondering how he was going to deal with them when the time came for explanations.

The crowd on the landing was anxious for details.

'I say, Jennings, what's going on?' demanded Venables.

'Nothing much. We found a famous Roman relic, only it's got stuck.'

'Bad luck. Still it's jolly decent of Mr Wilkins to help you move it.'

Offers of assistance poured in on Mr Wilkins. 'Let me have a bash, sir. I'm sure I could do it for you, if you'd let me,' begged Atkinson.

Mr Wilkins paused to mop his brow. 'No, thank you, Atkinson. I can get on much better without any help from you.'

'Well, would you like me to send for the fire brigade, sir? They're supersonic at getting people's heads free when they've got stuck between railings. We've got a big park at home with iron railings...'

'Will you be *quiet*, Atkinson? I have not got my head stuck between any park railings,' stormed Mr Wilkins, heaving at the wheel with all his might.

'No, sir, but you've got something stuck between the banisters and I thought...'

Atkinson broke off in wild alarm. For at that moment there was a rending of woodwork as the banister gave way under the strain and the wheel, suddenly freed, rolled headlong down the stairs.

Mr Wilkins made a grab to stop it, but he was not quick enough. With increasing momentum, it clanked and bounded down out of control, bumping from stair to stair and trailing its chain behind it.

'Look out. It's got loose!' yelled Temple. 'It's doing a jet-propelled take-off.'

'Stop it, Venables,' called Jennings from above.

'No, no, Venables – stand clear,' ordered Mr Wilkins.

Seventy-seven interested spectators darted for cover in all directions. Some scampered to safety along the landing; others slid down the banisters to the ground floor – and only just in time.

The wheel hit the bottom stair, lurched crazily – and then ran across the landing and smote the door of Mr Carter's study with a force that could be heard all over the building.

There was a moment of silence. Then the door opened and Mr Carter came out. He looked first at the fallen wheel, and then at Jennings and Darbishire hurrying down the stairs in pursuit of their rattling relic.

'Jennings!' he called sharply.

'Yes, sir?'

'Did *you* roll this thing down the stairs?'

'No, not really sir. I wasn't touching it at the time. You see, what happened...'

'Was it *you* then, Darbishire?'

'Oh, no, sir. I was standing well away from it when it went.'

Mr Wilkins' voice floated down from the bend on the staircase. 'It's all right, Carter. As a matter of fact ... well ... actually *I* did it.'

Mr Carter raised one eyebrow in surprise. '*You*, Wilkins... Well, really! What an extraordinary way to spend a quiet and peaceful Sunday afternoon!'

9

The Root of the Trouble

The afternoon which had started with such promise, ended dismally for the curators of the Form 3 Museum.

First, they were ordered by an indignant Mr Wilkins to lose, bury, destroy or somehow get rid of the object that was cluttering up the landing and making the building look like a Corporation refuse dump. Besides this, they were given a difficult French exercise to translate, and awarded two bad conduct marks for creating a disturbance during the Sunday quiet hour.

As they trudged sadly away with their clanking wheel, Mr Wilkins was busy making an entry against their names in the breakages book: – *Damage to staircase: Paint cracked, plaster chipped, one banister rail in need of repair.*

'What are we going to *do* with it?' moaned Darbishire, when they were safely out of earshot of Mr Wilkins. 'We can't take it all the way back to the Roman camp and bury it again.'

'I should jolly well think not,' Jennings

remarked warmly. 'After all, we discovered it, so it's ours. We'll just have to put it somewhere out of sight till Old Wilkie cools off a bit, and then we'll get an expert or someone to come and have a look at it.'

So they hid the wheel underneath a bundle of old potato sacks in the potting shed, and went indoors to start the French exercise.

By the time they had finished, Jennings had no heart left for the task of copying the entries from the exercise book into his little red diary. He would do it tomorrow, he thought, as he went upstairs to bed. After all, Mr Wilkins had said he could keep the diary until Monday evening.

Unfortunately the next day was a particularly busy one. The headmaster, Mr Pemberton-Oakes, was content as a rule to leave the day-to-day routine work of the school to his staff. But at odd and inconvenient times, he would suddenly decide to test the smooth-running organisation for himself. It so happened that he chose Monday for one of these investigations.

After breakfast, he held a shoe inspection. During morning break, he conducted a spirited attack on untidy tuck-boxes; fingernails were examined before lunch, and library books afterwards. At odd times during the day, the boys lined up for fire practice, choir practice, and inspections of pocket combs, textbooks and toothbrushes. Painstaking searches were organised for missing raincoat belts and indiarubbers.

And by the time Mr Pemberton-Oakes retired from the fray, their free time had all gone, and there were only a few minutes left before the dormitory bell.

What chance had he now, Jennings asked himself of writing his diary up to date before the time limit expired? However, he decided to make a start. He took the exercise book from his desk and scuttled along to the cloakroom to retrieve the diary from his raincoat pocket. On the way he met Mr Wilkins.

'I want that little red book back,' the master said. 'I said you could only have it until this evening.'

'Yes, sir; er – could I keep it just a *little* longer, please? Say till about teatime tomorrow, sir?'

'You've had it since Thursday – that's plenty of time. Haven't you finished it yet?'

'Well, I haven't actually *quite* finished, sir,' said Jennings truthfully. It sounded better than saying he hadn't yet started.

'H'm. I'll give you until after lunch tomorrow, and that's my last word,' said Mr Wilkins, as he strode off towards the dining-hall.

Jennings found his raincoat hanging on his peg in the cloakroom. He thrust his hand

129

into the pocket – and then into the other pocket; but the diary wasn't there!

He stood puzzling over the matter while a worried frown gathered on his brow. It *should* be there; he remembered taking it with him to the Roman camp. Perhaps he had put it in his desk or his tuck-box when he returned.

There was no time for a search then, for the dormitory bell was already sounding its shrill message. He went upstairs vaguely troubled.

By breaktime the next morning, he knew the diary was lost. With Darbishire's help he had searched every likely and unlikely spot in the building – behind the hot-water pipes, in the bootlockers – even under the pile of old sacks in the potting shed which shrouded their cherished museum piece.

During the afternoon, Venables came across the searchers going through the waste-paper basket in Form 3 classroom.

'Oh, there you are, Jennings! Old Wilkie's gunning for you. He came stonking into the tuck-box room like a square-dancing carthorse just now, and blew me up because I didn't know where you were.'

'Oh, golly! He wants my diary back. What on earth am I going to do?'

Venables pressed for details, and was told the whole sad story.

'It's no good telling him that you've lost it

now,' he observed, when the facts had been made plain. 'You should have told him last night when he asked for it, instead of making out that you'd still got it.'

'But I thought I *had* still got it then. I couldn't tell him I'd lost it until I knew myself could I?'

Venables shrugged his shoulders. 'Can't see Old Wilkie taking a feeble excuse like that. Whatever you say now, he's bound to think you lost it on purpose, so you wouldn't have to give it back.'

'Oh, fish-hooks, this is frantic! It's all very well for masters; when they lose cufflinks and things, nobody kicks up a hoo-hah, but just because I happen to...' he trailed off hopelessly.

'If you ask me,' said Darbishire, in tones which suggested that he wasn't expecting any one to ask him – 'If you ask me, I'd say you lost it at the Roman camp, so it's just a waste of time to go on wearing out our eyesight looking for it round these parts.'

It was a disturbing thought, but it seemed the most likely solution; the diary had probably dropped out of his pocket on the way home.

'In that case, you've had it!' said Venables decisively. 'Someone's bound to have picked it up by now. You'd better ask Mr Carter if you can ring up the police right away and see if it's been handed in.'

'I can't do that. I don't know the number,' Jennings demurred.

'You could easily find out. Ring them up and ask them,' suggested Darbishire brightly.

Jennings turned on his friend impatiently. 'Don't be such a bazooka, Darbishire. If I could do that I wouldn't *need* to ask them!' He paused for a moment, deep in thought. 'No, I'd rather go to the police station and explain things properly... You see, if that diary gets into the wrong hands – well, don't spread it about, but I'll have another packet of trouble coming my way – quite apart from any hoo-hah that Old Wilkie decides to kick up.'

They stared at him in surprise. They understood his worries about Mr Wilkins well enough, but what was this other trouble at which he hinted so darkly?

Jennings glanced round to make sure they were unobserved. Then he told them his problem.

The secret code was the root of it all. All those mysterious foreigners, *Selbanev, Nosnikta, Retsim Retrac*, and the rest, with their secret headquarters at *Yrubnil Truoc*: was there not a chance that the police might think they had stumbled upon a list of enemy agents? After all, Mr Carter had definitely stated that they sounded to him like members of an Eastern European Spy

Organisation ... and Mr Carter ought to know!

In his mind's eye, Jennings could see the scene at the police station when the diary was examined; a police sergeant compiling a list of the strange names to send to Scotland Yard's Special Branch. Only too well Jennings could imagine him thumbing his way through the diary and finding suspicious entries on every page.

What, for example, would be made of *Retsim Snikliw exploded atom bomb in Yrotimrod* on January 29th? How was anyone to know that this merely meant Mr Wilkins had been in an explosive mood when on dormitory duty?... What construction would be placed on *Erihsibrad hid secret plans under the Wollip?* (January 24th) – on the occasion when a list of arrangements for a midnight feast had to be hastily concealed on Matron's approach.

The idea of using the code for key words only had seemed a reasonable one at the time. But there was no escaping the fact that in the eyes of the law the entries would take on a new and sinister meaning.

Other instances came readily to mind. His private notes on the school timetable and curriculum, for example: *Down with Nital!... Llabtoof for ever!* (January 28th). Would it be thought that these innocent slogans smacked of treason and revolution?

Darbishire agreed that it would. 'It's just the sort of thing any decent spy would write in his diary,' he maintained when Jennings had finished listing his troubles. 'It's all very well writing things half in code and half not, to fox the masters; but whatever are the police going to think?'

'They'll understand if you go and explain right away, Venables urged. 'But if you *don't*...!' He gave a nod of deep significance. 'I can just imagine what the Head would say if he woke up in the morning and found Scotland Yard all over the football pitch, looking for *Retsim Snikliw* and the atom bomb plans.'

'Yes, the sooner it's cleared up the better,' said Darbishire. 'After all, if it gets about that *Erihsibrad* is really me in reverse gear – well, it'll take a bit of explaining, won't it?'

There were, then, several urgent reasons why something had got to be done. First and foremost was the impatience of Mr Wilkins for the return of the confiscated property; secondly, the embarrassment and misunderstanding that would follow if the diary fell into the clutches of an unsympathetic policeman. There was also a third reason: Aunt Angela's promised ten shillings could be written off as a total loss if the record of daily events was not kept up until the end of the year.

'All very well to say *do* something,'

grumbled Jennings. 'But I can't go waltzing off to the police station without permission; besides, there isn't time to walk all the way there and back before tea.'

That was the trouble with boarding schools, he always maintained; there were so many rules to hamper and thwart people with important jobs to do.

Here was a case in point: it was Tuesday afternoon, school was over and there was nearly an hour before tea. If only they were allowed out!... If only they were allowed bicycles!... If only...!

He ceased his catalogue of 'if only' as an idea flashed into his mind; not a very brilliant one, as ideas go, but at least it was worth trying.

'I know! I can borrow a day boy's bike,' he said. 'Pettigrew always stays on till after tea on Tuesdays, so how would it be if I went on his? I'll be back hours before he wants to go home.'

'But what about leave to go out?' said Darbishire, putting his finger on the flaw in the scheme.

Jennings' spirits sank. It would be hopeless to ask for permission to leave the grounds on a Tuesday afternoon. There was nothing for it but to abandon the idea altogether.

Just then the door opened and Mr Carter looked in. 'Volunteer wanted! Who would like to take some letters to post? I'm too busy to go at the moment,' he said.

'I'll go, sir; please let me go!' Jennings begged.

Here was his chance. Linbury Post Office was about ten minutes' walk from the school: a semi-detached villa marked *Sussex Constabulary* was a further quarter of an hour's journey on foot... But on a bicycle! – why he could post the letters, go and see the policeman, and still return in less time than it would take to walk to the village on his lawful errand.

He followed Mr Carter up to his study and collected the letters. Then he hastened along to the hobbies room to find Pettigrew, on whom his plan now depended.

Pettigrew was a plump, freckle-faced boy of twelve, whose fair hair hung down over his forehead like a fringe on a lamp shade. He lived near the village of Pottlewhistle on the Dunhambury Road; and nearly every day he and his friend Marshall, a lean and inky-fingered youth from Form 4, cycled to and from school together. Tuesdays was an exception; for then Pettigrew stayed to tea and preparation, and Marshall rode home alone.

'I say Petters, will you lend me your bike – just for half an hour?' Jennings urged. 'It's terribly important.'

Pettigrew was not keen, and summoned up all the reasons he could think of why such a loan would not be a practical proposition. 'It's got a slow puncture,' he objected. 'And there's not much battery left, and besides it's a bit tricky getting into bottom gear, unless you're used to it.'

Jennings demolished the arguments: 'That doesn't matter; I'll pump it up before I start back, and I ought to be nearly home by lighting-up time; and besides, I shan't use bottom gear anyway.'

'Oh, well – I suppose so,' said Pettigrew grudgingly unable to think of any more objections. 'What do you want it for, anyway?'

When he heard the reasons for the expedition, he became more enthusiastic. He was an imaginative boy and anything to do with police stations, spy hunts and secret codes stirred him deeply.

He led the way down to the bicycle shed, where a number of day boys were just leaving for home. The defective tyre was still quite hard, so they didn't waste time pumping it up. Jennings was instructed to attend to this before starting back on the return journey.

'Coo, thanks, Petters. It's ever so decent of you. I'm jolly grateful – honestly I am,' Jennings said, as he wheeled the machine out of the bicycle shed.

Darbishire had come along to wish him good luck and speed him on his way.

'Be careful, won't you, Jen,' he urged. 'You don't want to find yourself up a gum tree by getting mixed up in criminal proceedings and things.'

'Don't talk such antiseptic eyewash, Darbishire. It's just a straightforward matter about a lost diary – at least I hope it is.'

'My father says that if once you get on the wrong side of the law...'

'Oh, for goodness' sake! You're giving me the jitters – talking like a chronic old misery... Well, I'd better get cracking!' Jennings forced a smile: 'Don't you wish you were coming with me, Darbi?'

Darbishire shook his head. Painful memories of the last time he had set out on a bicycle made him only too thankful that he was being allowed to stay behind. Never again, he told himself as he went indoors, would he set out on an excursion as Jennings' cycling companion!

Pettigrew watched till Jennings had rounded the bend of the drive. Then, returning to the hobbies room, he met his friend Marshall coming down the stairs.

'Oh, there you are, Petters!' said Marshall. 'I've been looking for you all over the place. Do you mind if I borrow your bicycle pump? I'm in a bit of a hurry to get off.'

'Sorry, Marshy I've lent it to Jennings. He's just beetled off on a top priority secret important mission on my bike.'

'Oh, has he?... Well, he's gone without the pump then. I took it off your bike ten minutes ago.' He took the pump from his satchel and waved it in his friend's face.

'Well, I like the cheek of that!' protested Pettigrew. 'You never asked if you could borrow it.'

'I'm asking you now. You weren't about when I looked in the bike shed. I did try to find you.'

'Yes, but...! You are a coot, Marshall. You've bished up the issue properly taking it off without telling me,' Pettigrew complained.

He realised then, of course, that he ought to have looked to see that the pump was on the machine when he had been testing the doubtful tyre. But then, it had never occurred to him that it *wouldn't* be!

Pettigrew was indignant. This sort of thing was straining the bonds of friendship too far! 'Well, you can jolly well ride full pelt after Jennings and give him the pump back,' he said warmly. 'He doesn't know he's gone without it, and that slow puncture will just about be flat by the time he gets to the police station.'

'Police station!' echoed Marshall in surprise. 'Golly what's been happening?'

'Oh, nothing much. Jennings is just making a few private inquiries. If he's gone inside when you get there, leave the pump where he's sure to see it when he...'

'Yes, but what's he gone to the police for?' Marshall butted in excitedly. 'Private inquiries about *what?*'

Pettigrew had a lively imagination; and now he gave it full rein. 'Suspected espionage!... But don't tell anyone,' he whispered.

'Phew! You mean old Jen thinks he's on the trail of a spy?'

'Oh, no! He's afraid the police may think *he's* one. It all looks pretty black on paper, from what he tells me. That's why he wants to put himself in the clear before Scotland Yard start pouncing.'

'I say how wizard!' shrilled Marshall delightedly. Then he remembered how serious things were, and said hastily: 'I mean, poor old Jennings. I'm terribly sorry, really. Is there anything I can do to help him?'

'Yes, there is.'

'Oh, wacko – what?'

'You can jolly well take my pump along and make sure he gets it.'

'Oh ... is that all?' Marshall was disappointed. He had been hoping for a major part in what sounded like a fast-moving spy drama now nearing its climax. He put the pump back in his satchel and hurried outside to the bicycle shed.

140

10

Wrong Side of the Law

Jennings pedalled rapidly along the road to Linbury village. Now that he had actually started on his mission, he felt less happy about it than he had done before. There were so many 'ifs' and 'buts' to worry about. Would the police believe his story?... Supposing the diary had *not* been found... How then could he face Mr Wilkins? What would Aunt Angela say?... What if Mr Carter found out that he had borrowed a bicycle and gone farther than the Post Office?

With an effort, Jennings dismissed these disturbing thoughts. He must keep his mind on what he was doing, and his eye on the road ahead. Soon it would begin to grow dark. He would have to hurry, he told himself, if he was to complete his errand and get back in time for tea.

He stopped at the *Linbury Stores and Post Office* and slipped Mr Carter's letters in the box. Then he set off again on the second stage of his journey.

The nearest police station was at Dunhambury nearly five miles away; but a house with the notice *Sussex Constabulary* over the front door had caught Jennings' eye when he and Darbishire had made their ill-fated shopping expedition nearly three weeks before. It was here that the local constable lived. And with a growing sense of uneasiness, Jennings rode up to the front gate and dismounted.

He left the bicycle on the grass verge, made his way up the garden path and knocked on the door. He had nothing to worry about, he assured himself. He would tell the policeman what the code really meant and...

The door was opened suddenly by a tall, heavily built man of middle age. Was he the policeman, Jennings wondered? True, he was wearing dark blue trousers, but his tweed jacket and comfortable slippers seemed far removed from official uniform.

Jennings decided to play for safety 'I ...er ... I wish to speak to a policeman, please,' he said.

'Your wish is granted, sonny – I am a policeman,' the large man replied in a deep voice.

'Oh, good. Well, would you mind telling me whether anyone has given you a diary lately? As lost property I mean – not as a present,' Jennings explained, and then went on with a rush: 'You see, mine's disappeared, and what

I want to tell you is that, if anyone brings it to you, all that stuff about *Selbanev* and *Nosnikta* and *Retsim Retrac* and people – well, it doesn't mean what you think it means.'

'Oh, no! And what am I *supposed* to think it means?' asked the policeman, with heavy good humour.

'The Eastern European spy organisation, of course. You see, the diary says things like *Retsim Snikliw exploded an atom bomb in Yrotimrod one day last month.*'

The policeman stroked his chin thoughtfully. 'Dear me!... And didn't he?'

'No, not really,' Jennings gave a little, uneasy laugh. 'And all that about *Erihsibrad* hiding the secret plans under the *Wollip* – well, you'd laugh if you knew what the plans were... Just a few doughnuts and a box of dates after lights out, that's all.' Again the nervous laugh, as he glanced up at the policeman's face to make quite sure that he understood.

But Police Constable Herbert Stanley Honeyball was not at all sure that he *did* understand. He would, in fact, have admitted that he was floundering well out of his depth, and unable to make head or tail of this confused and jumbled rigmarole. All the same, he did his best.

'Now, look; let's get this straight,' he began. 'You've come to report the loss of a diary.'

'Yes, sir – er – I mean, yes, Constable.'

'Right; now, what's your name?'

Jennings hesitated. 'Well, strictly speaking, it's Jennings, but in the code, of course, it's *Sgninnej*,' he said.

PC Honeyball looked blank.

'It's the same with the others,' Jennings went on helpfully 'My friend, for instance – you'll find he's *Erihsibrad* backwards.'

'I'll find *who* is *what* backwards?'

'Darbishire. And the address, too. *Yrubnil Truoc Yrotaraperp Loohcs*.'

PC Honeyball looked even blanker. 'Are you trying to tell me that's a place in Derbyshire?'

'Oh, no!' Jennings smiled at the absurdity of such an idea. It was all so clear to him that it never entered his head that the police officer would have any difficulty in following what he meant. 'No, that's my address. Darbishire's not a place; he's a person. He's the person who said the place sounded like somewhere in Yugoslavia, but that was only a joke, of course.'

The constable blinked. He had failed so far to make sense of his young visitor's name; perhaps he would have more luck with his address. 'Where did you say you lived? Just repeat that address, will you?' he asked patiently.

'Oh, but it isn't my address really,' Jennings explained. 'Actually, I live at Linbury

144

Court School.'

'You said something quite different a minute ago.'

'Yes, I know But don't you see that's because it's all the wrong way round. *Yrubnil Truoc* is Linbury Court.'

PC Herbert Honeyball had had enough. Nobody was going to play practical jokes on *him* and get away with it!

'Now, look here, son – you've lost your diary. All right, I'll make a note of it. But I've no time for fun and games, and I don't like small boys trying to take a rise out of me,' he said. 'So run along and pull somebody else's leg for a change.'

'Oh, but sir – I mean, Constable! Look, you don't understand...'

Jennings found himself talking to a front door that was very firmly shut. He felt surprised and a little hurt. Perhaps the policeman hadn't understood properly. After all, it was a difficult business to explain, especially when one was feeling nervous and uncertain. Still, if the diary hadn't been found, there was no point in pursuing the matter further.

He retraced his steps down the garden path, and, as he walked through the gate, his foot kicked against a short cylindrical object propped against the gate post. He picked it up... It was a bicycle pump...

Marshall's instructions had been quite clear. He was to leave the pump where Jennings would be sure to find it. The safest course would have been to attach it to the bicycle; but when Marshall tried to do this, he found that the brackets would not hold the pump securely in position. What, then, should he do? According to Pettigrew, Jennings' interview with the police was likely to have sensational results. It might take a long time... Perhaps there would be statements to be made, evidence to be sifted, fingerprints to be taken... And Marshall wanted his tea...

So he placed the pump against the gatepost where it was bound to he noticed by anyone who came through. Then he mounted his bicycle and pedalled off home to the village of Pottlewhistle...

Jennings' expression was serious as he stood looking at the pump in his hands. It was extremely careless of someone, he thought, to lose a perfectly good piece of equipment like this. People ought to make sure that their pump brackets were in good working order before setting out on bicycle rides. Still the owner – whoever he was – could be thankful that his property had been picked up by an honest person who would do the decent thing, and hand it over to the police right away.

Some people had all the luck, he reflected

bitterly. Why couldn't his diary have been found by some equally honest citizen!

Jennings had a strong sense of public duty. He would return good for evil, and set a shining example of the way in which citizens ought to behave. He strode back up the garden path and knocked again at the front door.

Police Constable Herbert Honeyball was not pleased to see him.

'Now, look here, I thought I told you to run away,' he said sternly He was halfway through his tea, and he had no intention of letting his poached egg become spoilt at the whim of some youthful hoaxer.

'Ah, yes; but it's different this time,' Jennings assured him. 'I've come to report something I've found – not something I've lost.' He held up the pump for the policeman's inspection. 'Look, I found this – well, I bet you can't guess where.'

PC Honeyball said that it was unreasonable to expect a police officer whose poached egg was rapidly congealing to indulge in guessing games, especially when he had just gone off duty.

'Oh! Well, I'll tell you then. I was just going through your garden gate, and there *slap bang* on the path outside...'

'I'll book it down,' said Mr Honeyball shortly. 'What did you say your name was?'

'Well, my name's Jennings, but according

to that code I was telling you about, it's ... well, it's rather difficult to pronounce. Try saying...'

The policeman's patience was wearing thin by the time he had recorded the finding of a bicycle pump on the Dunhambury road by J C T Jennings of Linbury Court, at 4.52 p.m. approx. on the afternoon of February 16th... And by that time his poached egg was not worth eating.

Jennings had ridden barely five yards on his homeward journey when the bumping of his back wheel told him that his tyre was nearly flat... Of course! Pettigrew had said something about a slow puncture.

He dismounted and reached for the pump... It was some seconds before the explanation dawned on him, and even then there were still some things that he did not understand. Who was the crazy clodpoll, he asked himself angrily who had calmly removed the pump from its proper place and left it by the gate? No one but a stark, raving addle-pated half-wit would indulge in such senseless stupidity. A joke was all very well, but this was carrying things too far!

What on earth would Pettigrew say if he were told that his pump was now lost property?... What on earth would the policeman say if he were told that it *wasn't*?

Jennings' brow was ploughed with furrows

of anxiety as he made his way back through the gate and up the garden path: for he was not at all sure how the policeman would react to this new request. He hadn't seemed a very understanding sort of man; rather slow in the up-take, Jennings thought. After all, he'd been to a lot of trouble to explain how his code worked, yet the policeman hadn't seemed to follow it at all.

And now there was something else to explain! With some misgiving, he knocked for the third time at the police officer's door.

Herbert Stanley Honeyball had nerves of steel, yet he winced visibly when he saw who his visitor was.

'Cor, stone the crows! I thought I'd finished with you,' he began. 'Clear off, quick. I've no time for any more of your nonsense.'

'But it's not nonsense this time, really sir, er – Constable,' Jennings assured him. 'It's urgent. You know that pump I brought you just now?'

Mr Honeyball said he remembered the article perfectly.

'Well, I was wondering whether you'd very kindly let me have it back again.'

'If it's not claimed in three months, I'll send you a postcard.'

'Oh, but that won't be any good – I want it now. You see, it's – well, it's mine.'

A loud hissing sound, like steam escaping

149

under pressure, whistled through the constable's lips. Then he counted ten to give himself time to control his feelings before he spoke.

'...seven, eight, nine, ten. Now, look here, I've had enough of this carry-on. Strikes me you want your brain seeing to. If you brought that pump in as lost property it can't very well be yours, can it?'

'Well, you see, I made a sort of accidental bish, but it wasn't my fault. There's been an unknown hand at work: someone's tried to pull my leg – at least, I think he did, or why should he have taken it off and put it somewhere else?'

'What sort of a caper is this?... Who's taken *what* off *what?*'

'I was just trying to tell you that the pump's mine. It was all the time, only I didn't know it. After all, it's the sort of mistake that could happen to anyone, isn't it?' Jennings asked reasonably.

'Is it?' queried Mr Honeyball. 'There's not many as hand in their own possessions as lost property and then claim them back two minutes later... Well, if it *is* yours, has it got your name on it?'

'Oh, no; it hasn't got my name on. You see, it isn't mine *really*, that is...'

PC Honeyball was not light on his feet, but now he danced with frustration.

'Not yours? Not yours! Cor, stone the

crows, son – you just told me it *was!*'

Jennings felt that a more detailed explanation was called for.

'Well, actually it belongs to a chap called Pettigrew, but if anyone hands in that diary I was telling you about, you'll find his name's *Wergittep*.'

'Oh, yes; naturally it *would* be,' replied the police officer, with heavy sarcasm.

'Pettigrew's name, I mean – not the chap's who finds the diary. *Wergittep* is backwards, you see – like ... well, like *Retsim Snikliw* that I was telling you about.'

'Who?'

'Mr Wilkins – the one who exploded the atom bomb – only he didn't *really*, of course.'

'And he's the one who lost the pump, is he?' inquired Mr Honeyball, groping for some shred of reason in the tangle of explanation.

'Mr Wilkins? Oh, no; he's only got a link missing.'

'H'm! He's not the only one, either, I'd say!' muttered the policeman meaningly.

'You see, it was he who confiscated the diary and then let me have it back on loan; and I took it to the Roman camp on Sunday and...'

Jennings' voice trailed away. *Sunday* had just stirred a thought in his mind... Of course! He'd been wearing his best suit under his raincoat. That meant that, if he had put the diary in his jacket pocket, it was his *best* suit that he should have searched – not his everyday one... Yes, now he came to think of it, he could almost remember slipping the diary into his inside pocket just after he and Darbishire had finished the liquorice allsorts... Why hadn't he thought of it before!

A wide smile of relief spread over his face, and he turned to the bewildered policeman and said: 'Oh, wacko! I know where it is now. You needn't bother to make inquiries about it any more. Thanks all the same.'

Mr Honeyball said that it would be a great weight off his mind; but the sarcasm was wasted on Jennings.

'I'm ever so glad I came and told you about it, or I might never have remembered,' the boy prattled on. 'I do hope I haven't been wasting your time, sir – er, I mean, Constable.'

Herbert Stanley Honeyball took a deep breath. 'Oh, no; not at all; not at all,' he said, in a strained voice. 'Any time I'm off duty and in the middle of my tea, I shall be only too delighted to stand here in a perishing draught and listen to you blethering about atom bombs and secret plans and spies with unpronounceable names.'

'Well, I did my best to...'

PC Honeyball picked up the bicycle pump

from the hall table and waved it about in the air as though conducting a symphony orchestra.

'Cor, stone the crows!' he continued, on a rising note. 'And as if *that* wasn't enough, you don't know whether your own property is supposed to be lost or claimed, or even whether it is your own property at all!'

His patience, which had been wearing noticeably thinner in the last few seconds, now gave way under the strain. He ceased conducting his invisible orchestra and thrust the pump forcefully into Jennings' hands.

'Here, take your pump and go and blow up your own atom bombs with it – I've had enough of this lark!' he fumed.

The tea bell was ringing as Jennings parked Pettigrew's bicycle in the shed. He hurried indoors, just in time to join the end of the long line of boys streaming into the dining-hall for the evening meal.

'How did you get on?' Darbishire inquired busily passing platefuls of shepherd's pie along his side of the table.

'All right thanks. He hadn't got the diary but I think I know where it is.'

'Oh, good-o! I was a bit worried while you were out, I don't mind telling you. I didn't want you to get on the wrong side of the law.'

Jennings seized a slice of bread and butter from a fast-moving plate. 'Well, actually I'm afraid I *did*, in a way. He kicked up an awful hoo-hah just because – well, for no reason at all, really.' He shook his head sadly over the shortcomings of the police force.

From six places farther down the table, Venables sent along a verbal message: 'Pass down to Jennings that Old Wilkie's got him in his gunsights, and he's going to action stations after tea for a roof-level attack.'

It was quite clear what the message meant: Mr Wilkins was growing impatient for the return of the confiscated property!

Immediately after tea, Jennings rushed up to his dormitory locker to search through the pockets of his best suit: Darbishire went too, determined not to miss any sensational developments.

At first they had no success: Jennings' jacket was not in his locker. But Matron, interviewed on the landing, told him that he would find his best suit in the sewing-room where it was awaiting minor repairs.

'Oh, thanks, Matron... Come on, Darbishire!' They tore off along the landing at full speed, pausing only to take cover behind a dormitory door when they heard Mr Wilkins coming up the stairs, and loudly demanding to know if anyone had seen Jennings.

As soon as he had passed, they left their

hiding place and reached the sewing-room without further delay.

'Now, where's my jacket?' demanded Jennings, burrowing his way into a top-heavy pile of Sunday suits stacked on one of the shelves. The pile swayed, lurched forward into space and collapsed in a heap on the floor.

'Oh, fish-hooks – just when we're in a hurry too!' complained Darbishire. Patiently he started to re-stack the fallen garments, leaving Jennings to identify his own jacket from the knee-deep clutter of clothes about him.

The next moment, a shout of triumph rang out round the room, and Jennings was waving a small red book round his head.

'Got it... Hooray... How super-wacko-sonic!' He performed an ungainly ballet in celebration, and hurled a pair of Blotwell's trousers high into the air.

'Hey look what you're doing! We've got to put all this lot back,' Darbishire pointed out.

'Right-o! I'll give you a hand.' Jennings went in search of Blotwell's trousers which had fallen to earth behind a radiator on the far side of the room. As he pulled them out, he noticed a crumpled white shirt lying on the floor behind the hot pipes.

He picked it up, tossed it on to the back of a chair, and was moving away to help Darbishire, when a small, square object near the bottom of the sleeve caught his eye. He turned back and examined it with interest.

'I say Darbi!' he exclaimed excitedly. 'What do you think I've found in this shirt... Old Wilkie's missing link!'

'No!'

'I jolly well have. *Slap-bang-doyng* in the cuff of his shirt. Come and see for yourself.' He took the link from the shirt cuff and held it out for his friend's inspection. 'Old Wilkie's getting absent-minded in his old age. He kicks up a frantic hoo-hah and starts creating because he can't find it, and all the time he's forgotten to take it out of his shirt.'

'We're not doing too badly are we?' Darbishire observed. 'First we solve the mystery of the lost diary and then the riddle of the missing link. What are we going to come across next, I wonder?'

'Old Wilkie himself I'm afraid. I can hear him coming up the stairs,' said Jennings. 'Still, considering what we've found for him, he can't grumble much this time.'

'No, but I bet he'll have a jolly good try,' Darbishire muttered, as the sewing-room door swung back quivering on its hinges, and Mr Wilkins strode heavily over the threshold.

The master had had to ask fifteen people before he had been able to discover Jennings' whereabouts. He was not, therefore, in the sunniest of tempers.

'Jennings! What on earth are you doing in here?' His eyes ranged round the room, noting the untidy disorder of suits all over the floor. 'What's this – a jumble sale?' he demanded.

'No, sir, Matron said we could...'

'I'm quite sure Matron didn't say anything of the sort,' Mr Wilkins broke in. 'Tut-tut-tut! Suits scattered about like autumn leaves! What in the name of reason do you think you're playing at?'

'I just came in to get my diary, sir.'

The news did little to soothe Mr Wilkins' feelings.

'Oh, did you! And do you realise that I've been traipsing round the school looking for you? I told you to bring it back at lunch-time; that means *you've* to come to find *me*. I don't expect to have to walk round the building looking for you.'

'No, sir. I'm terribly sorry, sir, but I lost it,' Jennings glanced at Mr Wilkins and went on hurriedly: 'It's all right now, though; I've got it back. I went to an awful lot of trouble to get it for you, sir.' He placed the diary in the master's outstretched hand and then stooped to help Darbishire tidy the floor.

Mr Wilkins glanced at the little red book, and noticed that the cover would not lie flat. Some small object had found its way between the pages. He opened the book to remove the obstruction ... and there was his missing cufflink lying on the blank space reserved for April 1st.

There was no doubt that he was extremely surprised. For some moments he stared wide-eyed at the cufflink; and then his angry expression faded and gave way to a pleased, rather puzzled look. 'I ... er .. this cufflink. It's the one I lost, you know,' he said, in a voice unusually quiet for one of his blustery nature.

'Yes, sir. I just found it in your shirt behind the pipes,' Jennings answered.

'Did you? Did you, indeed? That was very clever of you, Jennings. Thanks very much.' There was a warmth and friendliness in his voice that the boys had not heard for some time.

'That's all right, sir,' said Jennings, embarrassed by this unusual display of good feeling.

'Yes, I'm more than grateful to get it back again, I can tell you,' Mr Wilkins went on, polishing the cufflink on his handkerchief. 'It was a twenty-first birthday present, you know.'

Darbishire decided the moment was ripe to drop a gentle hint. 'Of course, sir, we should never have found it if we hadn't been looking for the diary, should we, Jen?'

The hint was not wasted. 'No, I suppose you wouldn't,' said Mr Wilkins thoughtfully 'H'm! Well, in that case, I suppose the fairest thing I can do is to give the diary back in exchange.'

Jennings beamed. 'Oh, sir, thank you ever so much. Aunt Angela *will* be pleased, sir.'

'But no more funny descriptions of me, mind,' Mr Wilkins said warningly as he handed the book to the smiling owner.

'Funny descriptions?... Oh, but I never did, sir,' Jennings protested. 'All that about you and the missing link was just to remind me to...'

A sudden roar of laughter broke from Mr Wilkins' lips as he realised for the first time the true meaning of the entry. 'Why of course: how stupid of me... I'd forgotten you'd promised to make a note of it! And there was I thinking ... ha-ha-ha!'

Mr Wilkins was still laughing as he strode off along the landing in search of Matron. He would share the joke with her, he decided; she was just the sort of person to enjoy it. As he climbed the stairs, the hearty boom of his mirth resounded at full volume throughout the building.

When Mr Wilkins saw the funny side of anything, the news could never be kept secret.

11

The Genuine Fake

Mr Carter had not forgotten his promise to take a party of third formers to the Dunhambury museum; but it was not until some weeks after half-term that he was able to make arrangements for the visit.

Then, quite unexpectedly, a football fixture against Bracebridge School had to be cancelled at a few days' notice, and Mr Carter seized upon this chance to make use of a half-holiday free from other engagements.

The news was received by Form 3 with wild enthusiasm. Temple and Atkinson heard about it first, and went skidding into the common room after lunch, broadcasting the special news-bulletin at the tops of their voices.

'I say have you characters heard? We're going to Dunhambury museum on Wednesday with Mr Carter!'

'Gosh, how supersonic!' The crowd in the common room flapped their fingers with delight and whirled imaginary carnival rattles round their heads.

'Sit next to me on the bus, Venables?' asked Bromwich major.

'Right-o, Bromo! I vote we bag the front seat upstairs – just us two.'

'Hey, that's not fair! You can't bag seats in advance,' objected Martin-Jones.

'Yes, we can – can't we, Bromo! Just because you didn't think of it first, Jonah...'

The argument raged on, blithely ignoring the fact that the visit to the museum – rather than the bus ride – was the real reason for the excursion.

To Jennings and Darbishire, the journey presented a grave problem. If they were to take their chariot wheel to be examined by the museum experts – and it was unthinkable that they should go without it – might not Mr Carter refuse to allow them to take it on the bus? It seemed highly probable. And supposing Mr Wilkins came, too! His feelings about the chariot wheel were known to be unfriendly, his comments somewhat terse!

'Old Wilkie's bound to kick up a hoo-hah if *he* comes; he told us to lose it,' Jennings pointed out, as they discussed the matter in all its aspects.

Darbishire shook his head sadly over Mr Wilkins' lack of culture. 'Fancy expecting us to chuck historic remains on the rubbish dump. That's the sort of thing the Goths and the Huns and the Vandals used to do –

and you know what people say about *them!*'

'I shouldn't be surprised if Old Wilkie isn't a secret Goth, on the quiet,' Jennings replied knowingly. 'Or why should he be so keen on destroying Roman civilisation!'

It was useless to ask in advance for permission to take the wheel with them, they decided. On the other hand, if Mr Wilkins did *not* go...! And if Mr Carter was in a good mood...! Perhaps there was just a chance...!

They scampered off to the potting shed to prepare the wheel for its journey. They wanted it to be looking its best. After all, the curator of the Dunhambury museum wouldn't take kindly to muddy wheel marks and trails of rust all over his private sanctum. A quick dust with a handkerchief would take care of that.

They had only ten minutes before the bell was due to sound for afternoon preparation, so they had to work fast. Jennings threw off the potato sacks and started to scrape the rust from the hub with his pen-knife. Suddenly he stopped work and exclaimed: 'I say Darbi, there are some letters carved on the hub. You can see them, now I've got the rust off.' He narrowed his eyes and looked again. 'I can't make out the first one, but the other two are *BC.*'

'Must be the owner's initials,' Darbishire hazarded. 'Now, if it was *JC*, we'd definitely know it had once belonged to Julius Caesar.

I expect they were just as fussy in those days about having their private possessions properly marked as Matron is now.'

They knelt side by side, straining their eyes over the worn letters. The first one was so chipped and scarred by wear and tear that it defied all their efforts to puzzle it out. But there was no doubt about the two letters which followed. Darbishire muttered them over and over again – and all of a sudden a brilliant theory flashed into his mind. He uttered a wild yell of triumph.

'Wacko! I've got it, Jen! They aren't initials at all. *BC* is the date. Gosh, that *proves* it's a genuine relic if it was made in *BC –something.*'

'Golly Darbi, I believe you're right!' Jennings agreed, his eyes lighting up in excitement. 'Now we can go to Old Wilkie and tell him The words trailed away as the flaw in Darbishire's theory suddenly occurred to him. 'T't, t't! You *are* an ignorant clodpoll, Darbishire!'

'Well, I like the cheek of that! I stumble across the true facts, and all you can do is to call me...'

'Yes, but don't you *see!* It *can't* be the proper date, because when the chap carved those letters on the wheel he couldn't possibly have known it was *BC – something* at the time, could he?'

'Oh ... no, I suppose he couldn't.'

Darbishire was bitterly disappointed. The deduction had seemed to him a brilliant piece of reasoning, and he could not tear his thoughts away from the fact that he had so *nearly* made an amazing discovery. He continued to turn the matter over in his mind... Surely if the wheel did *not* belong to the *BC* era, why should the unknown carver have tried to pretend that it *did?*... Had they discovered a forgery?... If so, it must be a genuine Roman fake – something rare in the history of archaeology. By this time his theory was becoming a little confused, but he did his best to explain to Jennings what he meant.

'...so you see, if it's a *genuine* forgery that makes it a lot rarer, doesn't it?' he finished up.

'Does it?' said Jennings blankly. He had been unable to follow much of the closely reasoned argument.

'Well, of course it does. After all, they've probably got masses of genuine remains in the Dunhambury museum, but I bet they haven't got one where the Romans have been to the trouble of faking the date.'

They felt they had a strong case for taking the wheel with them on the following Wednesday. Mr Wilkins or no Mr Wilkins, they would do their utmost to have their opinion confirmed by the curator of the Dunhambury museum.

Mr Carter led the chattering crocodile of boys out through the school gates and halted them by the bus stop on the Linbury Road. There was only one other person waiting for the Dunhambury bus – a burly red-faced builder's labourer, laden with a pick-axe and shovel.

The bus was due in a few minutes, and Mr Carter checked his party to make sure it was complete. He ran his eye along the line from Venables and Bromwich major in the front, to Binns minor and Blotwell walking with Mr Wilkins at the rear.

Binns minor and Blotwell were not really entitled to go on the expedition, for they were both in Form 1: but Mr Carter had allowed them to join the party as they had been such keen workers for the Form 3 museum. *The Binns-Blotwell Collection of Possible Fossils* was much admired in the lower forms of the school.

So they had trotted down the drive one on each side of Mr Wilkins, asking him ceaseless questions in piercing, high-pitched voices.

'Please, sir, it's jolly decent of Mr Carter to let us come, isn't it, sir?' shrilled Binns minor.

'Yes,' said Mr Wilkins.

'Please, sir, you know Jennings' museum in the attic, sir?' squeaked Blotwell.

'Yes,' said Mr Wilkins.

'Well, sir, you know the sort of things he's got in it, sir?'

'I do,' said Mr Wilkins.

'Well, sir, please sir, will they have the same sort of things in this museum we're going to this afternoon, sir?'

'I sincerely hope not,' said Mr Wilkins.

'Why not, sir? Why won't they sir? And why do you hope they won't, sir?'

Mr Carter arrived at the tail-end of the crocodile. His check had shown that Jennings and Darbishire were not amongst those present.

'I can't think where they've got to,' he told his colleague. 'They were on the quad with the others when we started.'

'*Silly* little boys!' exclaimed Mr Wilkins. 'If they're not here in a minute they'll miss the...' He broke off as a distant rumble caught his ear.

At first he thought it must be the bus approaching, so he turned to look... And then stared in chilled amazement at the sight of the derelict contraption rolling out through the school gates, supported on each side by Jennings and Darbishire.

They were hurrying, fearful of missing the bus, and their speed caused the trailing chain to clatter and rattle like a shower of stones on a tin roof. As they drew near, it was seen that a luggage label had been fixed to one of the spokes of the wheel. In Jennings' best handwriting it said: *Passenger to Dunhambury – By Bus – This Side Up With Care.*

Mr Carter raised despairing eyes to the heavens, and Mr Wilkins tapped his foot with exasperation as the wheel rolled to a halt beside the bus stop.

'*Doh!* What do you mean by starting off on an organised expedition rolling that gruesome collection of scrap iron along the road?' he demanded.

'We have to roll it, sir – it's too heavy to carry,' Jennings pointed out.

'But what do you want to bring the thing *at all* for? You can't take an object like that on the bus. Roll it into the ditch and leave it there!'

'Oh, but, sir! We're taking it to the museum, sir. It's a historical relic, sir.'

'If it *was*, Jennings, we should be only too pleased to let you take it,' Mr Carter said. 'But as it's of no value whatever, I think we'll all get on much better if you leave it behind in the ditch.'

As he spoke, a double-decker bus came round the bend and drew up by the bus stop.

With heavy hearts, Jennings and Darbishire abandoned their relic on the grass verge. It was one thing to make hopeful plans – and quite another to carry them out.

There was no time now to convince Mr Carter: if he would not take their word for it, they would have to admit defeat... There is seldom anything to be gained by arguing with masters.

The builder's labourer boarded the bus, thrust his pick-axe and shovel into the space beneath the stairs and then went inside to occupy the front seat. Mr Wilkins led the way up to the top deck, with the Linbury party clattering happily up the stairs behind him. The last to ascend was Mr Carter; and before he had taken his seat, the conductor's hand was already moving towards the bell push.

But suddenly the conductor paused... He had seen a circular iron object with a label attached to it, lying on the verge. He had no time to waste in wondering what it was doing there. So far as he knew, it was some odd piece of equipment which the burly man had forgotten to pick up when he was stacking his tools under the stairs.

The conductor was a man of strength. With one powerful heave, he lifted the wheel on to the platform and set it down beside the shovel and pick-axe. Then he rang the bell.

His first inkling that he had made a mistake came when the burly builder wanted to get off at the next stop – and found that he could not disentangle his tools from the iron chain.

'You didn't ought to allow this old junk under the stairs – getting in everyone's way,' he complained.

'*I* didn't ought to allow it! Well, I like that! It's your junk, isn't it?' said the conductor.

'No. Nothing to do with me. Belongs to that party upstairs.' With a sudden jerk, the builder's labourer wrenched his pick and shovel free and jumped off the bus.

Things became more difficult after that. The wheel, dislodged by the convulsive heaving, refused to go back tidily under the stairs. With each lurch of the bus, it rolled backwards and forwards across the entrance to the lower deck, imprisoning the passengers within and the conductor without. The chain, also, caused some bitter argument, when a middle-aged clergyman got his heel caught in one of the links while attempting to alight from the platform.

It was some time before the conductor had pacified the passengers, and was free to go and collect his fares on the top deck. Then he approached Mr Wilkins who was sitting in the back seat.

'Are you the responsible person in charge of this party?'

'Yes, I'm one of them,' replied Mr Wilkins pleasantly. 'We want two adults and seventeen halves to Dunhambury please.'

'All in good time,' said the conductor. 'First of all, what's the idea of turning my bus into a junk yard.'

Mr Wilkins looked surprised. 'I don't

understand,' he said.

The conductor pointed down the stairs; and Mr Wilkins, distinctly puzzled, rose from his seat to see what the man was so concerned about. He soon found out!

'I... I... Corwumph!' he expostulated, as his eye lighted upon the well-known object, now rocking to and fro on the platform like a dinghy in a rough sea. He turned angrily to where the unsuspecting owner was sitting, three rows farther along the bus.

'Jennings! How dare you bring that – that monstrous contraption on to the bus. I distinctly told you to leave it behind.'

'But I did, sir.'

'You couldn't have done! It's rolling about all over the platform.'

'That's all right, guv'nor – *I* put it on,' the conductor explained. 'Thought it was wanted, see? It's the last time I'm doing any good turns for anyone. No one can't get on or off with that rusty old iron blocking up the gangway.'

'But it's a genuine antique,' Darbishire pointed out.

'So will my bus be a genuine antique by the time your old iron has scraped all the paint off.'

Mr Carter proposed a solution. 'Stop the bus and we'll take it off for you,' he suggested.

But by now they had left the country

behind and were in a built-up area with houses and shops bordering both sides of the road.

'Can't dump it here – not on the housing estate,' objected the conductor. 'Arrested for causing an obstruction, that's what you'll be. It'll have to stay where it is now until you get off and take it with you.' Muttering to himself about the folly of trying to do favours for an ungrateful public, he descended to the lower deck where he spent the rest of the journey helping stout passengers to squeeze past the obstruction on the platform.

Jennings and Darbishire felt that no blame could be attached to them for this new development. After all, they had not even known that their rattling relic was close at hand. So it was a little unfair, they thought, for Mr Wilkins to glare at them in an unfriendly fashion for the remainder of the journey.

But Mr Wilkins wanted a scapegoat, and Jennings was the obvious choice. 'You *silly* little boy. It really is too bad,' he complained, as the bus entered Dunhambury High Street. 'When we get back to school, Jennings, I'll... I'll... Well, you'd better look out!'

'Never mind, Jen,' Darbishire whispered. 'Old Wilkie will look a bit silly when the experts have seen it. I can't think why he bothers to come to a museum at all; he doesn't seem a bit interested in genuine archaeology and stuff.'

12

On View to the Public

The market town of Dunhambury is a place of some historical interest. It was founded by the Romans, pillaged by the Jutes, besieged by the Saxons, looted by the Danes, destroyed by the Normans and rebuilt by the Tudors. At various times it has been ravaged by fire, flood, plague and the death-watch beetle.

It is natural, then, that a town which boasts of such a colourful past should have a wide range of exhibits in its museum. These may be inspected daily between the hours of ten a.m. and four p.m. (one p.m. on Saturdays), Good Fridays and Bank Holidays excepted. Admission free.

The collection is housed some distance from the town centre; and as soon as the Linbury party had alighted from the bus, Mr Carter lost no time in leading them along the High Street, past the gas works, and into a tall stone building displaying the notice: *Dunhambury Borough Council – Museum and Art Gallery.*

All except Jennings and Darbishire. They

were told by Mr Wilkins, in very firm tones, that they must first find some quiet spot to dispose of their wheel and chain; after which they might join the rest of the party.

'Keep together, you boys,' Mr Carter ordered, as they made their way into the main gallery. 'If you go wandering around by yourselves, you'll miss half the exhibits.'

The boys were keenly interested in all they saw; Binns minor and Blotwell asked endless questions.

'Sir, please, sir! Mr Carter, sir! What are these things in glass cases, sir?' shrilled Binns minor.

Mr Carter stopped to look. 'Those are tools and weapons used by the Ancient Britons. That one's an axe, and those small pieces in front are flint arrowheads, found buried in the chalk. They only had very simple tools in those days, you know.'

A pause: then – 'But, sir, please, sir!'

'What is it, Blotwell?'

'Well, sir, if they only had bits of flint and stone and stuff, how did they manage to make such supersonic glass cases to put them in?'

Venables looked up from his inspection of an adjoining cabinet. 'I say Atki, they've got an antique iron comb here, with only three teeth in it.'

'What about it?'

'Well, it looks just like the one you lent me

174

to do my hair with before lunch.'

'Don't be such a coot – it's nothing like mine. My comb's got *four* teeth in it,' Atkinson pointed out.

The boys wandered round the gallery examining each showcase and comparing the contents with the exhibits in the Form 3 collection in the school attic. Then they passed on to the Roman gallery; and after that to the collection of mediaeval fowling-pieces and blunderbusses, used by the inhabitants of Dunhambury during the Civil War.

Mr Carter began to feel worried about the absence of Jennings and Darbishire. It was a pity that they should be missing so many interesting exhibits; after all, it was they who had inspired the excursion in the first place. He consulted his colleague.

'I can't think why Jennings and Darbishire aren't here yet,' he said. 'What exactly did you tell them to do?'

'I just sent them off in search of a rubbish dump or some place where they could get rid of their clanking monstrosity. I'm not taking that thing on any more bus journeys, thanks very much. They'll be along as soon as they've got rid of it; though, if you ask me, Carter, I'd say they don't deserve to be taken on an outing at all.'

Mr Carter felt a sudden qualm. 'You don't think they might try to bring it in here, do you?'

'What, in the museum? Good heavens, no!' Mr Wilkins laughed at the wild impossibility of such an idea. 'Why I can just imagine what the curator would say if they *did!*'

Jennings and Darbishire were doing their best to obey Mr Wilkins' instructions. It was bitterly disappointing to have succeeded in bringing their relic all the way to Dunhambury, only to be faced with defeat at the last hurdle. But they knew that there would have been no point in trying to convert the masters to their way of thinking.

'I thought Old Wilkie was going to blow up on the bus,' Jennings remarked, as they watched the party move off towards the museum. 'Honestly his eyes popped in and out like organ stops when he saw our famous remains *slap-bang-plonk* at the bottom of the stairs.'

'So did mine,' replied Darbishire. 'I thought I was seeing things. Of course I was, in a way but not the sort of things I was expecting to see, if you see what I mean.'

'Still, it was jolly decent of the conductor to bring it along,' Jennings observed. 'If he keeps a diary the same as me, he'll be able to put it down as his good deed for the day.'

They ranged themselves one on each side of the wheel and started off. They had no clear idea of where to take it, but they thought they would not have much difficulty in finding a suitable resting-place.

They were wrong! The centre of a busy town affords little refuge for cumbersome relics, and it was soon made clear to them by indignant shopkeepers that the wheel could not be left on private property. Discouraged, they moved on to the municipal car park, where the attendant, after one look of surprise, slapped a label on the hub and demanded sixpence as a parking charge.

'Oh, fish-hooks, no! We can't afford to pay for it,' Jennings protested. 'Besides, I haven't got any money anyway.'

After that, they went to the bus office and inquired whether they might leave a parcel until called for. The young lady gave her permission – and quickly changed it to a curt refusal when the 'parcel' clanked and rattled in through the door.

Then they tried the lost property office at the railway station – again without success; for the porter in charge told them he could not accept property that people *wanted* to lose.

During the next quarter of an hour, they were turned out of the recreation ground, refused permission to enter the park, and warned by a policeman for obstructing a pedestrian crossing. No one, it seemed, would let them leave it anywhere!

By this time they had acquired a following of interested spectators. Four small boys with loud voices, two little girls pushing an infant sister in a baby-carriage and an assortment of friendly dogs skipped along at the end of the trailing chain. The four boys shouted pointless remarks and shrieked with laughter at their own dazzling wit; the little girls giggled and simpered, and the dogs ran round in circles barking incessantly.

Jennings was in despair. He even thought of leaving the wheel in a telephone kiosk, but he had to abandon this idea as he was unable to find one that was empty 'This is hopeless,' he moaned, trying hard to ignore the interested spectators. 'There's just nowhere, is there? All very well for Old Wilkie to say go and dump it somewhere. I'd like to see *him* having a bash!'

They had stopped at a sign saying *No Entry* at the end of a one-way street. Darbishire took off his spectacles and polished them on the hem of his raincoat. Then he replaced them and studied the notice carefully.

'Better not go up there, Jen, or someone will start kicking up a hoo-hah,' he advised.

'Why? That notice means traffic. It doesn't mean people on foot.'

'Well, we *are* traffic – more or less. Anyone hearing us coming will think there's a fleet of cement-mixers or a lorry load of milk churns tanking up the road in bottom gear.'

Jennings looked round in search of

inspiration. Across the road was a tall stone building with a noticeboard outside. *Dunhambury Borough Council – Museum and Art Gallery*, it said.

'Gosh, look where we've arrived!' he exclaimed in surprise, and drew his friend's attention to the notice.

Darbishire nodded gloomily. It saddened him to think of all the others enjoying themselves inside the museum, while he and Jennings had to trudge round the streets in hopeless circles. Besides, it was all so unfair. Surely if anyone had the right to be included in the proceedings it was the founders of the Form 3 museum! 'And to think we could go in there, too, without this old wheel,' he mused.

Jennings made a sudden decision. 'Well, now we've got here, we'll go in *with* it. After all, that's what we came for, isn't it?'

Darbishire was appalled by the boldness of this plan. 'But what about Old Wilkie? If we go waltzing in we'll probably run *slap-bang* into him, coming round a corner. We shall be cloinking away like ten thousand dustbins, don't forget, and Old Wilkie's got supersonic earsight!'

'Wait here; I'll nip inside and see what's happening.'

Picking his way through the ranks of the spectators, Jennings crossed the road and hurried into the museum. In front of him was the main gallery. A few visitors were wandering round, but there was no sign of the school party, so he went through into the second gallery which housed most of the Roman remains excavated from the camp-site near the Dunhambury road.

At the end of this room, a notice directed visitors to other parts of the building. By turning left, one reached the mediaeval section, and the exhibition of local arts and crafts; the corridor to the right led to the curator's office and the art gallery.

Jennings took the left-hand turning; but he had not gone far before he caught sight of Temple peering intently at a cannon ball in a room at the end of the corridor. Then the sound of Mr Wilkins' voice delivering a lecture on mediaeval blunderbusses was wafted down the corridor, and Jennings turned and hurried back along the way he had come, and out of the building.

He knew now what he must do. If they acted promptly there should just be time to take their museum piece along to the curator's office, while Mr Carter's party was studying ancient artillery, and admiring the local arts and crafts.

Darbishire was still standing glumly on the corner, drumming his fingers on the spokes of the wheel. The interested spectators had drifted away by this time: and it was just as well they *had*, Jennings thought; it was no part of his plan to have a disorganised rabble trailing into the museum behind them.

'It's all right, Darbi; they're all in a room at the far end, listening to Old Wilkie spouting about fossilised fowling-pieces, or something. If we're quick, we can beetle along to the expert's office without running into our crowd at all.'

Hurriedly, they rolled their rumbling ruin across the road, and bumped it over the door step, through the entrance hall and into the gallery beyond. But the next stage of the journey was not so easy as Jennings had hoped. The floors of the museum were made of highly polished oak, and, with no carpet to muffle the vibration, the noise of the iron-tyred rim and the rattling chain sounded deafening in the hushed quiet of the main gallery.

The room was empty as it happened, but it was obvious that it would not remain so for long when once the barrage of sound reached the ears of an attendant.

'Ssh!... Ssh!... *Quietly*, Darbi!' Jennings implored, with an urgent grimace of caution.

'What do you mean, *Ssh?* It's not *me* making the noise. It's this old contraption you've got to start *shush*-ing.'

They halted, aghast at the noise they were creating. Something would have to be done, Jennings decided. Why they wouldn't last ten seconds at this rowdy rate of progress!

The idea came to him in a flash. 'I've got it, Darbi. We'll slide it. Hang on to the spokes while I take my coat off!'

In a matter of seconds he had folded his raincoat into a bulky pad which he placed on the floor under the iron tyre. Then he gripped the spokes and slid the wheel along the highly polished floor on its makeshift cushion, while Darbishire trailed along behind holding the chain clear of the ground, like a train-bearer in a royal procession.

In this way they passed noiselessly into the Roman gallery, took the turning to the right and stopped outside the office of the curator. Jennings knocked.

'Come in,' said a precise voice from the other side of the door.

Mr Adrian Hoyle, the curator of the Dunhambury museum, was a tall, cultured, scholarly looking man in his fifties, with mild blue eyes and receding hair. He was vaguely surprised when the door of his office shot open and an antiquated object, cushioned on a raincoat, came sliding in, propelled by two breathless small boys.

The floor-polishing party skidded to a halt before the curator's desk.

'Good afternoon, sir. We've brought something to show you,' Jennings began. 'We thought you'd be interested as you're an expert, and know all about Roman remains and things.'

The curator blinked and smiled modestly. 'I can hardly claim to know *all*,' he said in his dry, scholarly voice. 'Though I have a certain – ah – reputation in archaeological matters.'

'Well, can you tell us whether this is a genuine forgery or not? We dug it up on the old Roman camp.'

'The *Castra Romanum*, you know,' added Darbishire. It sounded more impressive in Latin, he thought.

Mr Hoyle rose from his chair and regarded the object through half-closed lids. 'H'm... M'yes... Tut-tut... Dear me... Well, well... Fancy that, now... H'm,' he murmured.

Jennings craned forward eagerly. 'You – you think we've really *got* something, sir?' he breathed.

Mr Hoyle rubbed his ear thoughtfully. 'You've certainly got *something* – I'm just wondering *what*.'

The two boys exchanged hopeful glances. There could be no doubt of the rarity of their find. Why even the expert was puzzled!

'Could you tell us how long it's been buried, please sir?' Jennings asked.

'Well, it's not possible to be really accurate in cases like this,' Mr Hoyle answered. 'But I should say that this – ah – this object last saw the light of day some time round about the end of the war.'

'Gosh!... Caesar's Gallic War?'

'Oh, no, no – the last war.'

'What!'

'Mind you, I may be a year or so out in my estimate, but somewhere around nineteen forty-five would be a reasonable conjecture for the date of it's – ah – interment. The date of manufacture, of course, would obviously be some years earlier.'

There was a shocked silence. Then Jennings said: 'Oh, fish-hooks! That means it isn't ancient at all – perhaps not much older than me, even.'

'Precisely,' observed Mr Hoyle. 'It has reached a more advanced state of decay of course, owing to the interment to which you have – ah – fortunately not been subjected.' He permitted himself a scholarly smile at his little joke, but his idea of humour was lost on Jennings and Darbishire.

'So I suppose that means it's not even slightly valuable?' Jennings persisted.

'As a museum piece, no. Though I have no doubt that a scrap-metal merchant might value it at two or three shillings.'

The two boys stared at him with glazed eyes, unable to believe this verdict which shattered all their hopes. Surely it couldn't be true!... The thrill of discovery, the pride of ownership, the hazards of the journey even – was it possible that these were worth nothing?... Well, not more than two or three shillings, anyway!

Darbishire came out of his trance. He had just remembered something.

'Yes, but look, sir. It's got the date stamped on it. Of course, we knew it couldn't be the right date – that's why we thought it must be a genuine forgery.'

He pointed to the worn initials on the hub. What would the expert make of *that*, he wondered! Perhaps, now, he would be obliged to admit that he had made a mistake, and apologise for his rash judgement.

Mr Hoyle bent down and made a further inspection. 'H'm... Yes... The first initial is indistinct, but I should imagine it was the letter *D*. The letters *BC* immediately following, clearly stand for Borough Council.'

He straightened his back and went on in his dry, precise tones: 'As an archaeologist, my studies have largely been confined to the history of Roman Britain, and I am not really qualified to express an opinion on objects – ah – interred at a later date. But I would say that you have discovered a cartwheel and part of the brake chain of a vehicle used by the Dunhambury Borough Council, prior to the war, for the purpose of transporting sand and gravel and – ah – miscellaneous material of that kind... How it came to find a resting place on the campsite is beyond me to explain.'

Again there was silence. Finally Darbishire said: 'Oh... Oh, I see! Well, thank you very much for telling us anyway, sir.'

'Not at all! I'm only too pleased to have been able to help you,' smiled Mr Hoyle.

As though in a dream, they turned and made their way out of his room. They were half-way down the corridor when they heard him calling them back. There was a certain urgency in his tone.

'One moment, please! There's just one thing I'd like you to do before you go.'

They made their way back to the door. 'Yes, sir?'

'You might take your – ah – collection of municipal old iron with you,' suggested Mr Hoyle reasonably. 'I really don't want my office littered with the remains of the Borough Surveyor's sand and gravel cart.'

If proof were needed of the state of their feelings, this was it! Only minds unnerved by disaster would have left the relic – and the raincoat – in such an unsuitable place.

Outside in the corridor once more, Jennings leaned heavily against the wheel, and spoke his mind. 'Well, this is the most supersonic bish since the Battle of Bannockburn,' he said bitterly. 'All the trouble we've been to – and Old Wilkie was right all the time. It's jolly well the last time I'm ever going to dig up remains.'

'But what are we going to *do* with the thing

now?' wailed Darbishire. 'If it's only come off a dustcart or something, it's no good even for the Form Three museum. And, anyway, Old Wilkie would never let us take it home on the bus.'

Jennings shrugged his shoulders hopelessly. 'We'll have to leave it here, then.'

Darbishire was horrified. 'What!... Here in the museum!'

'There's nowhere else, is there? If we bung it in the Roman gallery with all those javelins and things, no one will ever know the difference – except the curator, of course. After all, it *looks* like a genuine Roman chariot wheel, doesn't it?'

It was a desperate measure; but once decided upon there could be no going back. They wasted no time. In less than a minute, the wheel was leaning against the wall of the Roman gallery between the spear of a centurion and a fragment of a fourth-century hypocaust.

It was barely in position before footsteps sounded along the corridor, and the Form 3 expeditionary force traipsed back through the gallery on their way out. By this time they had seen everything – except the bogus chariot wheel; and fortunately the entire party hurried out into the entrance hall without noticing this new addition to the Roman gallery.

Mr Carter was pleased to see that Jennings

and Darbishire had arrived at last. 'Where on earth have you been?' he demanded. 'You've missed everything worth seeing; we're just going to catch the bus home now.'

'Well, sir, it was that wheel. Mr Wilkins told us to get rid of it.'

'And did you?'

'Oh yes, sir. I think it will be quite all right where we've left it, sir.'

'Thank goodness for that,' chimed in Mr Wilkins, with deep feeling.

It was time then, to make their way back to the bus stop; and Venables and Bromwich major led the party out of the building to line up on the pavement outside. Mr Wilkins paused in the doorway, as his eye lighted upon a small kiosk selling picture postcards and handbooks of the museum.

'You take the boys on, Carter, and I'll join you by the bus stop,' he said. 'I'd rather like to buy one of these handbooks, if I can find an attendant to serve me.'

It was a decision which he was to regret bitterly before many minutes had elapsed.

13

Mr Wilkins Rides Alone

Mr Wilkins waited by the kiosk for a little while, but no one arrived to attend to his needs. Then he saw a notice informing visitors that an attendant could be summoned by ringing a small bell on the counter. Mr Wilkins rang the bell, but still no one appeared.

He was just on the point of abandoning his quest for the handbook when the door of the main gallery behind him swung open, and a tall, scholarly man, with mild blue eyes and receding hair, came hurrying through.

He paid no attention to the customer at the kiosk, but hastened out into the street, where he stood peering to left and right. Finally he came back into the entrance hall, his scholarly brow creased with a worried frown.

Then he saw Mr Wilkins, and said in dry, precise tones: 'Excuse me, did you happen to notice any boys leaving the museum recently?'

'If you mean the party from Linbury

Court School, they went some minutes ago. They'll be half-way to the bus stop by now,' Mr Wilkins answered. 'Is there anything I can do? I'm one of the masters in charge.'

'You are!' A look of hope dawned in the mild blue eyes. 'This is most opportune. You're just the person I wish to see. I am the curator of this museum.'

'Oh, really! How d'you do. My name's Wilkins. I was hoping I might get a chance to meet the curator. I'm rather anxious to buy a handbook, but I can't find anyone to serve me.'

There was no answering smile on the face of Adrian Hoyle as he said: 'Would you mind stepping this way Mr Wilkins. There is something in the Roman gallery which might be of interest to you.'

'Splendid!' replied Mr Wilkins heartily. He followed the curator through the main gallery to the Roman exhibits beyond. He was chatting in a jovial, light-hearted manner as they went through the door. 'We've examined this Roman section pretty thoroughly of course; and I must say some of the things you've got in here are most interesting. I know all the boys enjoyed themselves enorm...'

The flow of words stopped as abruptly as a disconnected telephone call as his eye lighted upon a familiar object propped up against the wall. His eyebrows rose, his jaw

190

dropped, and he stared in horrified amazement at this latest addition to the collection of Roman remains.

Then speech returned. 'I... I... Corwumph... It's – it's unbelievable!'

'Precisely,' observed Mr Hoyle.

'It's – it's monstrous!'

'Exactly,' concurred Mr Hoyle.

'It's – it's that boy, Jennings!'

'That, of course, I wouldn't know; he didn't mention his name,' said Mr Hoyle. 'Perhaps, however, you can explain why this irresponsible young person in your charge has chosen to exhibit a disused cartwheel, belonging to the Dunhambury Corporation, between a fragment of a fourth-century hypocaust and the spear of a Roman centurion.'

'I... I... Well, I'm terribly sorry of course. I told the boys to dispose of it.'

'In the Roman gallery?'

'Good heavens, no! I had no idea he'd do anything so fatuous. Now, of course, the wretched child has gone off, and there's no time to fetch him back before the bus goes.'

Mr Wilkins glanced at his watch; it was later than he had thought. He would have to hurry or he would miss the bus himself.

'Please accept my deepest apologies, Curator. I'll look into this matter as soon as I get back to school and, believe me, I'll see that the boys concerned are dealt with in no uncertain manner.'

He turned to make his way out of the gallery – only to find the gangway blocked by a very determined curator.

Adrian Hoyle was mild-mannered by nature, but when roused he could stand his ground in the fearless manner of the Roman centurions whose relics he guarded with such care.

Patiently, but firmly he said: 'I have no doubt, Mr Wilkins, that you will deal at a more suitable moment with the culprits concerned in this – ah – regrettable escapade. In the meantime, however, I shall be obliged if you will remove this – ah – collection of scrap metal from the precincts of the museum.'

The gallery swam before Mr Wilkins' eyes. He clutched at a showcase for support – and hurriedly let it go again as it tottered dangerously on its spindly legs.

'What – you mean you want *me* to take it away?' he gasped.

'Immediately – if you will be so kind,' returned the curator in the same tone of polite firmness. 'I insist upon its instant removal. I can't allow it to remain here a moment longer.'

'But ...but where can I take it?' protested Mr Wilkins helplessly 'I can't calmly abandon rusty iron wheels up and down the High Street. Do, please, be reasonable!

Where on earth am I to put the thing?'

'That, I'm afraid, is a matter for you to decide. As curator of this museum, I have the right to demand that it shall be removed forthwith.'

Mr Hoyle had been feeling strongly on the matter ever since that distressing moment, shortly after the departure of the boys, when he had emerged from his sanctum and entered the Roman gallery. To his horror he had found a party of American tourists admiring the bogus exhibit under the impression that it was the spare wheel of Queen Boadicea's war chariot. It was then that he had hurried outside in search of the culprits – and had found Mr Wilkins.

But the curator was not the only person who was nursing strong feelings. Mr Wilkins, too, was in the grip of a powerful emotion; most of which was directed at Jennings and Darbishire, now trotting happily towards the bus stop without a care in the world.

It was too late now, to call them back; the bus would be due at any moment, and in any case there was little to be gained by such a course. He made one last desperate appeal. 'Yes, but look here, I can't possibly...'

The curator cut him short: 'You have just admitted, Mr Wilkins, that you are one of the adults in charge of the party. The responsibility for the instant removal of this

'– ah – object, therefore, rests with you.'

'Yes, I know but I... I... Dash it... What I mean is...!'

'At *once*, if you please, Mr Wilkins. The museum closes in precisely three minutes from now.'

Adrian Hoyle was courteous to the end. He steadied the wheel while Mr Wilkins took a reluctant grip on the spokes; he held open the door of the Roman gallery while Mr Wilkins struggled through; and he went out on to the museum steps and watched as Mr Wilkins, pink to the ears with embarrassment, trundled the unwieldy, rattling relic along the street.

It took the straggling crocodile of third-formers some time to make its way back to the bus stop at the town centre. Apart from the difficulty of threading its way in and out of the shopping crowds thronging the pavements, the crocodile had frequently to be halted so that Blotwell could catch up with the main body.

To Mr Carter, he explained at great length that his inability to walk any faster had nothing to do with the shortness of his legs. It was, he declared, due to the fact that Binns minor had spent the afternoon dropping cannon balls on people's toes, while pretending to admire mediaeval artillery. If Mr Carter cared to look closely, Blotwell continued, he would observe that he, R G Blotwell, was obliged to walk with a pronounced limp.

Binns minor denied the charge strongly. 'Oh, I didn't, sir! I only dropped one once, by accident, sir,' he protested, his face flushed with outraged innocence. 'And Blotwell was miles and miles away at the time, sir – you ask anyone.'

'No, I wasn't! I was quite close, and it jolly nearly landed *slap-bang-wallop* on my left foot.'

'Well, if it only jolly nearly landed on your left foot, why do you have to limp with your *right?*' Binns demanded triumphantly

Blotwell glanced hurriedly down at his feet to see which one had the pronounced limp; then he changed his halting gait over to the other foot. He still felt that more sympathy should be shown to people who had jolly nearly had a painful accident.

'Come along, Blotwell, catch up with the others,' ordered Mr Carter. 'We shall miss the bus if we're not there in a couple of minutes.'

They were *not* there in a couple of minutes. Venables and Bromwich major led the hurrying procession round the corner into the busy High Street just in time to see the bus disappearing in the direction of Linbury.

Mr Carter's comments on people suffering from reasonably narrow escapes from cannon balls were inclined to be terse. The half-hour's wait before the next bus was due meant that the party would be late for tea when they arrived back at school.

The boys were delighted. They went out so seldom during term time that they were more than content to stand round the bus stop for half an hour, watching the traffic pass by – provided, of course, that there would still be some tea left when they got back.

'Pity you missed seeing all those things,' Temple said to Jennings. 'In one room we went into, they've got some supersonic blunderbusses that they used round about William the Conqueror's time – or perhaps it was a bit later. Anyway Old Wilkie told us they used them for bombarding the enemy with grapefruit. You wouldn't think it possible, would you?'

'Oh, I don't know,' Jennings replied, trying to conjure up the scene of battle in his mind's eye. 'I suppose a good hearty *zonk* with a ripe grapefruit would keep the enemy quiet while you were loading up with cannon balls and things.'

'You're stark raving bats, both of you,' Atkinson chimed in. 'Old Wilkie said grape-*shot* – not grape*fruit*.'

'Oh, did he? Well, it's all the same, isn't it?'

Blotwell approached Mr Carter. 'Sir, Mr Carter, sir! It's a jolly good thing I had to limp really because Mr Wilkins would have missed the bus otherwise, wouldn't he, sir!'

It took Mr Carter a few seconds to deduce Blotwell's meaning. 'You mean we should have caught it and he wouldn't. Yes, that's quite true, Blotwell.' He glanced at his watch: it was certainly taking his colleague a long time to buy that handbook!

'Isn't Mr Wilkins coming back with us, then, sir?'

'Oh, yes; I expect he'll be along any minute now,' Mr Carter replied.

His prophecy proved correct. No sooner had he spoken than a shattering barrage of sound thundered along the High Street towards them. Nervous shoppers leapt like startled deer, and anxious mothers hustled small children into the shelter of shop doorways. All along the street, heads popped out of windows, and pedestrians paused in mid-stride, curious to know the cause of the deafening tumult. And at the bus stop, seventeen bewildered boys stared open-mouthed and wide-eyed as the missing member of the Linbury party clattered self-consciously along the road towards them. Behind him pranced four small boys with loud voices, two little girls pushing an infant sister in a baby-carriage, and an assortment of friendly dogs.

It was clear that Mr Wilkins was not enjoying his stroll in the afternoon sunshine. On leaving the museum, he had at first tried to look as though he had no connection with the object in his care. He had worn an air of aloofness, suggesting that it was the merest chance that he happened to find himself going the same way as the rattling contraption by his side. But the amused stares and unkind comments that greeted him, soon made him abandon this pose, and after that he had pressed forward doggedly with gritted teeth and firm-set jaw. Things had been bad enough in the side streets, but now that he had reached the main thoroughfare, his embarrassment became even more acute. Fortunately he had not much farther to go; he squared his shoulders, took a fresh grip on the spokes and rattled his way along the High Street at a brisk four miles an hour.

The excitement at the bus stop was considerable.

'Gosh, look at Old Wilkie! He's found Jennings' famous relic.'

'What's he want to bring it along here for?... Everyone's staring like blinko.'

'Perhaps he's changed his mind, and decided that Jennings can keep it after all.'

'Jolly decent of him, if he has. Old Jen will be ever so pleased.'

Binns minor and Blotwell hopped from

foot to foot in hysterical excitement – until Blotwell remembered his unfortunate injury: after that, he hopped on one foot only.

Mr Wilkins rattled to a halt by the bus stop. His countenance was a deep purple, his eyes were smouldering with indignation, and for a moment he was too overcome to speak.

But Mr Carter wasn't.

'Well, really, Wilkins,' he exclaimed, in tones of shocked surprise. 'I thought we'd safely got rid of that fearsome object. Why ever do you want to bowl it along the High Street like a hoop?'

'I *don't* want to bowl it along the High Street like a hoop!... You don't imagine I'm doing this for my own selfish pleasure, do you?' snorted Mr Wilkins, as the power of speech returned. 'It's those wretched boys, Jennings and Darbishire. Just wait till I get back to school!'

'I'm terribly sorry, sir,' Jennings apologised. 'You see, I didn't know where else to put it, and I thought it would be all right there, because it sort of matched everything else.'

'Be quiet, Jennings! You've caused enough trouble for one afternoon,' complained Mr Wilkins. Then he turned swiftly to cope with the crowd of interested spectators at his heels.

'Go away, you inquisitive children. *Go away*, will you!... And take those bounding hounds with you.' And such was the wrath in his tone that they went without a word of protest.

But the wheel and chain still remained, and the problem of their disposal was as acute as ever. They could not leave it in the middle of the High Street – the experience of Jennings and Darbishire had already proved that to be out of the question – and Mr Wilkins was firm in his refusal to take it on the bus. Not for a long time, he maintained, would he forget the embarrassment he had felt when the passengers on the lower deck had had to scramble their way out like fugitives from a chain gang.

Finally, Mr Carter said: 'There's only one thing for it; we'll have to take it back to school by taxi, and get rid of it when we get there.'

'Good idea, Carter – it's the only way,' Mr Wilkins agreed. 'And what's more, Jennings and Darbishire can pay for it. I shall deduct five shillings from their pocket money as soon as we get back to school... Now, where can I find a taxi?'

Mr Wilkins marched off in search of a cab rank; and then Mr Carter decided that, as they were certain to be late for tea, it would be as well for him to telephone Matron, so that she could make the necessary arrangements with the kitchen staff.

'Wait here, you boys; I'm just going over the road to make a phone call,' he said.

'But supposing the bus comes, sir?' queried Venables.

'It isn't due for quarter of an hour; I'll be back in a couple of minutes.' And Mr Carter crossed the High Street and disappeared into the post office.

Comment flowed freely now that both masters were out of earshot.

'Wow! You've done it this time, Jennings – you haven't half dropped a clanger with Old Wilkie!' Atkinson observed.

'Yes, and that's nothing to the clanger he won't half have dropped by the time the Head gets to hear about it,' added Bromwich.

'Serves you jolly well right, if you ask me,' said Temple. 'I've met some crazy coots in my time, but I reckon Jennings and Darbishire take the certificate of merit for first-class cootishness, any day.'

'We couldn't help it. What else could we do?' protested Darbishire. 'I'd like to see some of you chaps doing better!' One way and another the afternoon had not been a success for the founders of the Form 3 museum. And Darbishire's feelings were bitter. It was most unfair. Why he asked himself, did these ghastly hoo-hahs always have to pick on *him* to happen to! And then there was this new worry about finding the money to pay for the taxi. It was all very well for Mr Wilkins to talk about deducting five shillings from their pocket money; but it was doubtful whether their combined bank balances could meet such a demand.

He confided his doubts to Jennings. 'I'm down to my last eightpence. How much have you got?' he inquired.

'About one-and-ten, I think.'

'Oh fish-hooks! That means we shall be half-a-crown short, so I suppose there'll be another hoo-hah about that.'

He stared at the traffic with hopeless, unseeing eyes. Amongst the cars and bicycles was a pony cart moving slowly towards them, close by the kerb. The driver, a small man with a hoarse voice, was shouting what appeared to be some sort of native war cry. The words were difficult to distinguish, and such was Darbishire's gloom that he failed either to notice the small man, or to understand the meaning of his strident shouts.

But Jennings still had all his wits about him. Suddenly he seized his friend by the arm. 'Listen, Darbi. That chap with the pony cart.'

'Well, what about him?'

'Can't you hear what he's shouting?'

Darbishire inclined an ear towards the traffic. To him the cry sounded like *En-yo-*

lion ... rags-er-bols...!

'No; *I* don't know what he's chuntering about. He might be singing "Pop Goes the Weasel" for all I know.'

'Don't be so dim, Darbi! He's a junk man – he's shouting for old iron and rags and bones and things.'

'What about it?'

'Well, how would it be if we asked him...?'

'Gosh, yes!' Darbishire burst out suddenly as he caught the drift of Jennings' idea. 'He *might*, mightn't he? After all, the curator did say it was worth a few shillings.'

The pony cart was level with them now. By straining an ear, it was just possible to follow the little man's war cry. 'Any old iron ... rags or bottles?'

Jennings waved wildly. 'Hey just a minute. Would you like to buy a wheel and chain. I'm afraid it's not a genuine antique, of course, but it's very heavy.'

The junk man had already spotted it. He stopped the pony and jumped off the cart. 'Is it yours?' he demanded suspiciously.

'Oh, yes, it's ours, all right – I'm afraid. That's what all the trouble's about,' said Jennings.

The little man ran an expert eye over the relic. Then he felt the weight; the heavy links of the chain seemed to give him great satisfaction.

'Plenty of scrap there – heavy enough to

sink a battleship. Give you three bob,' he offered.

'Oh, that's jolly decent of you, but half-a-crown will be enough, thanks all the same,' said Jennings modestly. He felt it wouldn't be right to make a profit on the transaction.

'Right y'are, son. Cash down on the nail!' The coin changed hands.

Form 3 had been following the course of the sale with keen interest. Now they came crowding round to help the junk merchant to lift his purchase on to the cart.

'Come on, let's all help,' called Venables. 'Wow, isn't she heavy... Altogether now: one, two, three – *heave!*'

There was a loud thud as the wheel and chain landed in the cart. Then the little man jumped on to the driving seat, stirred up his pony and passed on down the street.

They had seen the last of the rattling relic. 'Well, that was a bit of luck,' smiled Jennings. 'That means we've got five shillings now, altogether – just enough to pay for the taxi.'

'Only just in time, though,' observed Darbishire: for at that moment a taxi, with Mr Wilkins seated inside, came swerving round the corner, and pulled up at the bus stop with a screeching of brakes.

Mr Wilkins stepped out on to the pavement. 'Where's Mr Carter?' he asked.

'He's just coming out of the post office,

sir,' said Temple, pointing across the road.

'Good! I'll have to get him to give me a hand...' Mr Wilkins broke off, puzzled. He looked up and down the street, unable to find the object which he sought. 'That's funny – where is it?' he demanded.

'The wheel, sir? Oh, that's all right – I've just sold it, sir,' said Jennings.

'Sold it!'

'Yes, sir. A rag-and-bone man gave me half-a-crown for it.' Proudly he held up the coin for the master's inspection. Then, with equal pride, he showed it to Mr Carter who had just made his way back to join the group.

'You see, sir, Darbishire and I needed another half-crown to pay for the taxi, sir.'

Mr Wilkins clutched his forehead in both hands and leaned against the taxi for support. 'I... I... Well, I'm...! Of all the...! Why couldn't you have done this before I *got* the taxi?'

Jennings turned to Mr Carter for support. 'Haven't I done right, sir?' he inquired.

Mr Carter sighed patiently. 'What Mr Wilkins means, Jennings, is that, now you've disposed of your wheel, we no longer need the taxi to take it home in.'

'Oh, I see!' He gave a little, nervous laugh. 'No, of course, we don't need the taxi after all now, do we, sir!'

Mr Wilkins laid a restraining hand on the

door of the vehicle. 'Oh yes, we *do* need a taxi! I am going back to school in it; and what's more, I'm not taking any silly little boys with me.'

'But you could come back with us on the bus, sir,' Atkinson pointed out.

'Thank you very much for the suggestion, Atkinson, but I don't propose to do anything of the sort. I have just made a firm resolution that nothing will induce me to break.'

'What's that, sir?' asked Temple, with interest.

'I have just resolved,' said Mr Wilkins, 'that from now on I shall never undertake a journey by bus, if it means travelling on the same vehicle as either Jennings or Darbishire.'

14

Knotty Problem

The ink-splashed pages of Jennings' diary shed an interesting light on the events of the last few weeks of the Easter Term. The record, here, is easier to follow, for the secret code was abandoned, with deep regret, in case it should lead to further awkward misunderstandings.

The visit to Dunhambury is mentioned – (March 10th) *Went to Mus. on bus saw some things Mr W took taxi* – but there is no account of the uncomfortable quarter of an hour in the headmaster's study which followed their return to school.

There are records of 'Good Days' – (March 20th) *Baked beans had bath and piano lesson won match no prep wizzo –*... And 'Bad Days' – (March 27th) *Maths test Mr W in bate feeble semolina pudding lost match jolly mouldy*. Also on record are details of the arts and crafts exhibition, organised by Venables, who had been deeply impressed by what he had seen at the Dunhambury museum – (*Made clay ashtray for Ven also pipe-rack*).

But, although the day-to-day record was

maintained, Jennings could never find time to copy in the entries from the green exercise book he had used when the diary was in Mr Wilkin's possession. He often *meant* to start this formidable task, but somehow it never got done, and the term drifted to its close while the exercise book lay gathering dust on the attic shelf, and fifteen empty spaces remained in the little red diary

It was due to this neglect that the term nearly ended on a note of turmoil and confusion – *nearly* but not quite!

The last afternoon before the boys went home found Matron busy packing trunks in the dormitories, Mr Wilkins busy adding up marks in the staff room – and Jennings busy practising the piano in the music room next door.

Silvery Waves was a tuneful melody composed of lilting trills and resounding chords. Mr Hind, a softly spoken master who taught history in lower forms and music throughout the school, had been coaching Jennings in the piece for some weeks. So far his progress could be described as only fair.

The first dozen bars he could manage well enough, but then came the difficult bass chords which caused him so much trouble... And that afternoon they troubled Mr Wilkins, too, when he found himself obliged to add up his marks to the sound of *Silvery*

Waves repeated over and over again in the adjoining room.

Tiddle-om-pom ... thump ... tiddle-om-pom ... thump... Tiddle-iddle-iddle-iddle-om-pom... A pause; and then came a discordant crash like a tea tray dropped on a tiled floor.

The walls of the music room were by no means soundproof. Mr Wilkins patiently endured the crashing tea trays for some time, but at last he threw down his pencil in despair.

'It really is too bad, Carter,' he complained to his colleague. 'Every time that wretched little boy reaches that bar of music, he plays the wrong note – five or six wrong notes by the sound of it.'

'I didn't realise you were such a stern musical critic,' Mr Carter said, with a smile. 'You'll get used to it by the time he's finished his practice.'

'It's all very well for you to treat it as a joke – you've finished adding up *your* marks; but I've got the whole of Form 3's marks in history, geography and maths to do yet, *and* their places in form to work out, too. And every time that boy strikes that horrible discord he puts me off and I lose count.'

Tiddle-om-pom ... thump... tiddle-om-pom ... thump! sounded loudly from the adjoining room.

He picked up his pencil and started all over again, his lips moving silently as he muttered the numbers over to himself. 'Fifteen and twelve are twenty-seven and eighteen makes forty-five...'

Tiddle-om-pom ... thump... tiddle-om-pom ... thump!...

'...forty-five and three are forty-eight and twenty-seven are – er, um – seventy-five, and...'

Tiddle-iddle-iddle-iddle-om-pom.

'... seventy-five and fourteen make...'

Crash!

'Oh, good heavens, he's done it again! Tut-tut-tut. That's the fourth time I've lost count, and I'd got up to seventy-something, too. How on earth can anyone be expected to add up marks with some uncouth youth hammering the piano like a blacksmith's anvil.'

Once more he began: 'Fifteen and twelve are twenty-seven and eighteen makes forty-six – er, no, forty-five and three makes...'

Tiddle-om-pom ... thump ... tiddle-om-pom ... thump...

Silvery Waves began to get on Mr Wilkins' nerves. He found himself waiting for the crash that he knew was sure to come... Then he found himself humming the tune of '*Silvery Waves*' and sometimes even singing the numbers in his mark book as he added them up.

Tiddle-om-pom ... thump ... tiddle-om-pom ... thump...

This wouldn't do at all, Mr Wilkins thought to himself. He couldn't afford to waste a moment: all the other masters had finished writing their reports and adding their marks, but he had been so busy with end-of-term activities that he had only recently had a chance to get to grips with his mark book. And the headmaster was waiting for Form 3s results, and had twice sent to the staff room to see whether they were ready.

'...seventy-five and fourteen are eighty-nine and seventeen make a hundred and six...'

Tiddle-iddle-iddle-iddle-om-pom... Crash!

Mr Wilkins leapt to his feet.

'I'm going to put a stop to this, Carter! Music practice or no music practice, I can't have that fearful noise going on – I'd got up to a hundred that time, too!'

He strode out on to the landing and into the music room. The *tiddle-om-poms* stopped in mid-trill as he entered.

'Oh, so it's you, is it, Jennings – it *would* be! What are you doing in the music room?'

'Playing the piano, sir.'

'I can hear that, you silly little boy – except that it sounded more like *tuning* the thing than playing it.'

'Mr Hind said I was to make up the half-hour I missed on Saturday, sir, so I thought I'd come and do a sort of famous, last, end-of-term practice now, sir,' Jennings explained.

'Oh, did you! Well, I'm adding up my famous, last, end-of-term marks, and if I hear any more of that noise while I'm doing them, there'll be a famous, last, end-of-term rumpus. You can come back after tea when I've finished, and do your practice then.'

'Yes, sir.'

Jennings picked up *Silvery Waves* from the piano and added it to his untidy pile of music books on the floor beside him. Then: 'Where shall I put my music, sir? Mr Hind said nothing was to be left in the music room because it's been tidied up for the holidays, and the Head's coming round to inspect it before tea, sir.'

'Give the books to me, then,' the master replied. 'They can stay in the staff room till you want them for your practice, and after that they will have to be packed in your trunk.'

'Yes, sir... And what shall I do now, sir?'

'*Do!*' echoed Mr Wilkins impatiently. 'I don't mind what you do. You can stand on your head for all I care, so long as you don't disturb me while I'm working.'

He returned to the staff room and tossed the pile of music on to a chair. Now perhaps he could work in peace. With a frown of concentration, he bent his head over the green exercise book in which he kept the records of the term's marks in his subjects.

'Twelve and fifteen are twenty-seven and eighteen makes forty-five and three makes forty-eight and twenty-seven are seventy-five...'

From the next room came a sudden thump, followed by a discordant clash of notes as though some bulky object had been spread-eagled over the keyboard of the piano.

'*Doh!*...What on earth's the silly little boy playing at *now!*' fumed Mr Wilkins, losing count of his marks for the eighth time.

This time, it was Mr Carter who went to investigate. He found Jennings picking himself up from the music room floor; globules of dried mud from the soles of his shoes were scattered about the piano keyboard.

'What on earth are you doing, Jennings?' Mr Carter demanded.

'Please, sir, Mr Wilkins told me to stand on my head, sir.'

'Mr Wilkins told you to – *what?*'

'Yes, sir; he gave me permission just now, but I overbalanced and made a sort of forced landing on the piano, sir.'

With a patient sigh, Mr Carter explained that the whole point of postponing the piano practice was so that Jennings should go as far away as possible from the music room, and find something to do in another part of the building.

'But there *is* nothing to do, sir,' Jennings pointed out. That was the queer thing about the end of term, he always maintained; everybody was too excited to settle down to do anything, with the result that they became bored because they had nothing to do.

Mr Carter made a suggestion. The exhibits in the Form 3 museum were still spread out in the attic. Would it not be a good plan to tidy the room and dispose of any of the articles which were no longer needed?

'Coo, yes; supersonic wheeze, sir! I'll get Darbi to help me.'

Jennings went in search of Darbishire, whom he found packing his tuck-box in the basement. He had packed it, unpacked it and repacked it several times a day during that last week: it made the end of term seem a lot nearer, he claimed.

Together the two boys mounted the stairs to the attic and set about the task of tidying up. First, they played marbles with the *Binns-Blotwell Collection* of possibly-fossilised smooth round stones; then, they buried the seaweed and the shrivelled starfish under a loose floorboard, so that they would know where to find them the following term. Behind the collection of old bottles found on the beach, Jennings came across the clay models he had made during hobbies hour for Venables' exhibition of arts and crafts.

'Oh, I must take these home with me,' Jennings said, as he picked them up. 'They'll make jolly decent Easter presents for my mother and father, won't they?'

Darbishire peered at the craft work through dusty spectacles. 'What are they meant to be?' he inquired.

'Well, this lumpy one's an ashtray for my mother; and this spindly sort of gadget is a clay pipe-rack I could give to my father.'

'Does he smoke a clay pipe, then?'

'Oh, no; it's not a special rack for clay pipes– It's a rack for ordinary pipes made out of clay, if you see what I mean,' Jennings explained. 'Of course, my father only smokes cigarettes really; but still, a pipe-rack's quite a decent thing to have, isn't it?'

'Wouldn't it be better to give him the ashtray if he doesn't smoke a pipe?'

Jennings pondered the suggestion. 'Yes, but then I'd have to give my mother the pipe-rack; and that's no good, because she doesn't smoke.'

'Well, what does she want an ashtray for, then?' Darbishire demanded.

'So she can lend it to my father, of course. Honestly Darbi, you've got no idea of choosing decent presents for people.'

Clutching the fragile objects carefully Jennings made for the door with the intention of taking them along to his dormitory and packing them in his trunk. Half-way across the room, he paused as his eye lighted upon a green-covered exercise book tucked away at the back of the shelves.

'Golly I forgot all about this! It's the manuscript of part of my diary, that I wrote when Wilkie had confiscated the proper one. Lucky I spotted it! I'll take it home and copy it in during the holidays.'

The tea bell sounded just then, so Jennings decided to postpone the packing of his Easter gifts until a more convenient time.

But after tea he was detailed to take part in a search for missing library books. This kept him busy downstairs for some while, so he did not know that Matron was hard at work in the dormitory cramming the last items from his clothes locker into his already overfull trunk.

'I shall need a strong man to close the lid,' she remarked, when she had finished.

'Let me have a bash, Matron – I'm a strong man,' volunteered Temple, who was going round the dormitories scraping the remains of old luggage labels from the trunks. He hurried to her assistance, and they knelt one at each end of the trunk, straining to close it. But even so, their combined efforts failed to shut the lid against the pressure of the contents inside.

Mr Wilkins walked by the open dormitory door. He was feeling more cheerful by this time for he had finished adding up his marks shortly before tea, and now he was on his way to the staff room to retrieve his mark book and take it along to the headmaster's study.

'Can I give you a hand, Matron?' he inquired pleasantly.

'Thank you, Mr Wilkins – if you'd be so kind. It needs a strong man on the job.'

Mr Wilkins smiled modestly. A strong man! Why, she had asked the very person!

'Right, let's have it in the middle of the room where we can see what we're doing.' He heaved the trunk clear of the floor and staggered a few steps away from the foot of the bed. 'By jove, it's heavy! Whatever's the boy got inside it – cannon balls? It feels as though it's lined with lead, and brass-bound at the corners.'

'I expect it's his football boots at the bottom, sir,' suggested Temple.

'Urr – gurr... Corwumph,' strained Mr Wilkins, setting the trunk down with a thud.

'Don't hurt yourself,' Matron cautioned. 'I only want it closed – you needn't bother to carry it around.'

'It's going to be a job to shut this – probably need grappling irons, or something,' Mr Wilkins remarked doubtfully as he slipped off his jacket. 'I'd better put some rope round it, too: these locks aren't much good.'

Temple was sent off to ask Mr Carter for a coil of rope. He left Mr Wilkins kneeling on the lid, *corwumph*-ing with exertion.

'Phew! I wouldn't like this job too often,' he complained. 'Ah! – that's got one end shut.' He transferred his weight to the other end, bouncing up and down on the lid with the full weight of his fourteen stone in an effort to compress the contents of the trunk still further.

'Oh, do be careful, Mr Wilkins! Either you or the trunk will collapse if you go on like that,' said Matron. She watched anxiously fearful lest at any moment he might go through the lid, or the hinges snap under the strain.

The last catch had just been forced into position when Temple returned with the rope. Behind him came Jennings clutching his Easter gifts, and Darbishire balancing the green exercise book on his head.

'Oh, sir! You've fastened it already,' Jennings exclaimed, in troubled tones.

Mr Wilkins mopped his brow and loosened his collar. 'Yes, and it took some doing, I don't mind telling you.'

'Oh, but, sir, I'm awfully sorry but would you mind opening it again?... There's some more to go in yet.'

'Would I mind I ... I most certainly *would*

218

mind,' the master objected with some heat. 'I'm not opening this trunk again for all the tea in China.'

'But what about my presents, sir? You see, there's my mother's ashtray for my father to use because he won't need a pipe-rack and she doesn't smoke...'

'Well, they're not going in here, and that's that,' Mr Wilkins said firmly. 'It's over-flowing and bursting out in all directions as it is: and what's more, I've done enough weightlifting acts and square-dancing per-formances on trunk lids to last me for some time.'

'Oh, sir,' said Jennings, aggrieved.

'And you other boys!' Mr Wilkins turned impatiently on Temple and Darbishire. 'What are you hanging about for?'

'I just came to watch, sir,' said Darbishire.

'Came to watch! What do you think this is – a television show? Run away both of you, and find something useful to do.'

'Yes, sir.'

Mr Wilkins picked up the rope and started on the second stage of the operation. The coil was a long one – long enough to be wound lengthways and crossways round the trunk several times: and Mr Wilkins threw himself into the task with all the energy at his command.

'When I tackle a job, I like to ... do ... the ... thing ... properly,' he gasped, straining to lift the trunk into a more convenient position. 'If a job's worth doing, it's worth ... doing ...well,' he panted, setting his burden down heavily.

No one could say that L P Wilkins, Esq., was not thorough. Round and round, across and over, back and forth he threaded the rope, securing it at each crossover with a workmanlike assortment of knots. There were clove hitches in the middle, bowlines on bights at each corner, sheet-bends above and timber-hitches below. He used up the last inches of the coil by tying two reef knots and a rolling hitch, which he threw in for good measure.

'There,' said Mr Wilkins, straightening up from his task, some ten minutes later. '*That* won't come undone in a hurry!'

'I'm sorry for your mother, Jennings, she'll have a terrible time undoing all those knots,' Matron observed, as she hurried out to pack more trunks in another dormitory.

Mr Wilkins chuckled. 'She'll know I wasn't in the Scouts for nothing,' he remarked, as he put on his jacket.

Perhaps the busiest member of the staff on that last evening was Mr Carter. He had checked the boys' travelling arrangements for the following day and given them their railway tickets and pocket-money. Now, he was making a tour of the building to see that it was tidy and that no private possessions had been left behind. He arrived in Dormitory 6, bearing a list of some two dozen items that needed attention.

'Ah! There you are, Wilkins,' he remarked, as he came through the door. 'Have you finished your marks and final places for Form 3?'

'Yes, I've got them all worked out. They're in an exercise book on the staff room table,' his colleague replied. 'I was just going to take them along to the Head's study when Matron asked me to give her a hand.' He moved across to the mirror to straighten his tie and smooth his hair. He had not spared himself in his battle with the trunk, and his appearance had suffered as a result. For some moments he was too busy making himself tidy to pay much attention to what was happening elsewhere in the room.

'Right! Now, what else is there to be seen to?' Mr Carter consulted his list... *Atkinson – football boots missing... Bromwich major – Cough mixture... Binns minor – No belt on raincoat... Jennings...*

'Oh, yes, Jennings – your music! The headmaster says you're to ask your mother to make sure you do your piano practice every day during the holidays.'

'Yes, sir,' said Jennings.

'You've packed your music, of course?'

A look of alarm passed over the boy's face, and his hand flew to his mouth in guilty realisation. 'My music! Oh gosh! No, I haven't, sir. I'm awfully sorry; I forgot all about it, sir.'

Mr Carter frowned. 'Where is it?' he inquired.

'It's still in the staff room, sir. Mr Wilkins put it there when he stopped me doing my practice; and then I forgot all about it, sir.'

'You really are an infuriating boy Jennings,' Mr Carter said. 'Why couldn't you have brought it up earlier!'

'I'm terribly sorry, sir... What had I better do, sir?'

'Go and get it at once, and slip it in your trunk before it's locked. It's too big to go in your suitcase.'

It was clear that Mr Carter was not abreast of the latest developments in Dormitory 6. With some misgiving, Jennings filled in this gap in his knowledge.

'That one's mine, over there, sir,' he said, pointing to the well-trussed trunk. 'It's locked already. Mr Wilkins has just done it.'

At the mention of his name, Mr Wilkins, trim and tidy again now, looked round from studying his reflection in the mirror.

'What's that about me?' he inquired.

'I was just telling Mr Carter that you've locked my trunk, sir.'

'I certainly have. And I've made a pretty thorough job of it, too, I can tell you,' Mr Wilkins said, with justifiable pride. He glanced at his handiwork and gave a little chuckle of satisfaction. 'By jove, I'm sorry for the person who has to open it.'

For one fleeting moment, the ghost of a smile haunted the corners of Mr Carter's mouth. Then gravely he said: 'In that case, you'd better start feeling sorry for yourself, Wilkins.'

'Eh! Why's that?'

'Because your next job will be to untie all those knots so that Jennings can pack his music... The headmaster is most insistent that he takes it home for the holidays.'

15

Jennings Tries his Hand

Mr Wilkins clasped his hands to his head and ran distracted fingers through his hair. 'Oh, *no*, Carter, not *that!*' he protested. 'It's too much to expect me to go through that all-in wrestling business a second time.'

'I'm sorry but it will have to be done. The Head's rule is that music must be packed flat in trunks, and not screwed up into bundles and crammed into suitcases,' his colleague pointed out.

'Well, I... Of all the... You really are a *silly little boy*, Jennings!'

'Yes, sir; I know, sir; sorry, sir,' Jennings mumbled. And then, seeing a faint ray of hope in the gloom of the disaster, he said: 'Of course, sir, if you've got to open it again anyway, couldn't you squeeze my Easter presents in, too, sir?'

'No, I could *not!* I don't even know how we're going to get the music in, as it is.'

Mr Wilkins bent over the trunk and tugged fiercely at the nearest knot – which seemed to bind more tightly the harder he pulled. It did nothing to improve the state of his feelings to see that Jennings was standing idly by, watching his progress with a detached air.

'Well, don't stand there staring at me like a half-wit! Go and fetch the music – and be quick about it!'

'Yes, sir.'

On his way downstairs to the staff room, Jennings met Darbishire, still wearing the green exercise book on his head like a crownless mortar board.

'Old Wilkie's in a mouldy bate, just because he's got to open my trunk again to pack my music,' Jennings told him. 'And on top of that, he won't let me put my Easter presents in.'

'I shouldn't think there'd be much room on top of that. Won't they go in underneath?'

'No, you clodpoll! I mean he won't let me put them in at all. I shall have to make a parcel and carry them; and I didn't want to do that, because my mother's sure to spot them when she meets me, and I was hoping to give her a surprise.'

'She'll get that all right when you tell her that the thing like a china nest egg is really an ashtray.'

Jennings ignored the criticism of his handiwork. 'Yes, but I've got one parcel already,' he explained, as they trotted along to the staff room together. 'I found some rather supersonic junk in the waste-paper basket after we'd cleared our desks out, so I thought I'd take it home.'

'Anything decent?' Darbishire inquired, with interest.

Jennings shook his head. 'Not really; I shall probably bung it all in the dustbin when I get home, but it seemed a pity just to leave it in the waste-paper basket.'

His friend nodded in agreement. 'Yes, it would only get thrown away wouldn't it?'

By this time they had reached the staff room door. They received no answer to their knock, so they hurried inside and began to hunt round for Jennings' music.

It was not surprising that it took them some time to find it, for the staff room on the last evening of term was the one really untidy room in the whole building. Stacks of textbooks, loose sheets of exam paper, and old chalk boxes filled with india-rubbers, were piled high on the table and overflowed on to the floor. Deflated footballs were heaped in one corner, boxing gloves and linesmen's flags in another, so that the room looked more like a derelict lost property office than a quiet retreat for gentlemen with academic leanings. But it was only on the last night of term that the staff room housed this motley collection of jumble; for by then the other rooms had been tidied and all the doubtful objects which had no place of their own somehow found their way to the staff room, to add to the discomfort of the masters.

'Wow! What a ghastly old junk shop,' Jennings exclaimed, as he picked his way round in search of his music. 'That's just like masters: they blow up like atom bombs just because, say you leave your blotch slightly skew-whiff inside your desk, or if, perhaps, your ruler's two inches out of place – and all the time their own room looks like a ransacked warehouse.'

Darbishire laid the green exercise book down on a pile of atlases, while he inspected a box of confiscated property he had spotted on the floor. It was not often that he found himself free to roam round the staff room, and he determined to make the most of it.

'I say Jen, look! Here's Atki's old water pistol that Mr Carter confiscated at half-term. I've often wondered what masters do with all the things they take away from us. Seems a bit of a waste just to bung them in a box, doesn't it?' He delved deeper into the stock of confiscations. 'Oh, look, here's the golf ball that I dropped when the Head was making a speech about not fidgeting in roll call... Well, I never thought I'd have the pleasure of seeing *that* again!'

Jennings had found his music by this time. As he straightened the sheets, a thought occurred to him. 'I say Darbi, where's that exercise book you had, with all those things I've got to copy into my diary?'

'It's about – somewhere. I only put it down half a minute ago. What d'you want it for?'

'Well, I could easily bung it in with my music: Old Wilkie would never notice and he'd have to pack it then, wouldn't he?' He glanced round and saw what he thought was his exercise book next to a sheaf of exam paper on the table. 'Oh, yes; here it is!' He picked it up and slipped it inside the covers of *Silvery Waves*.

It was unfortunate that both Jennings and Mr Wilkins should have made use of school stationery for their own purposes. For the Linbury Court exercise books had similar covers, and it was only too easy to pick up a wrong book by mistake.

'Come on; let's get this music up to the dorm before Old Wilkie starts gunning for me,' Jennings said. 'He's not in the sort of mood to be kept waiting.'

He led the way upstairs, quite unaware that the manuscript of his diary still lay on top of the pile of atlases, and that Form 3's marks for the term in history geography and mathematics were reposing between the pages of *Silvery Waves*.

Mr Wilkins was undoing the last of the

workmanlike knots when Jennings and Darbishire returned to Dormitory 6. He had removed his jacket and rolled up his sleeves; his tie was crooked, his hair was awry; his fingertips were sore and his temper was ruffled. He was heartily tired of trunks, of forgetful small boys, and of bowlines on bights.

'Come along, Jennings; hurry up with that music,' he said. 'I don't want to spend the whole night in this dormitory.' He unwound the rope, and slipped back the catches of the trunk. The lid flew open, the contents ballooning upwards as the pressure was relieved.

'And what do *you* want, Darbishire?' Mr Wilkins demanded. 'I told you once to go away. What do you think I'm doing – providing free demonstrations for your entertainment?'

'Oh, can't I watch, please, sir? I like watching people packing trunks,' Darbishire said chattily as the master rammed the music books hard down on top of the bulging contents. My father's awfully good at shutting trunks that won't shut, sir. What he does is to...'

'I've no doubt he does, Darbishire: but I'm doing this my own way thanks very much.'

Jennings fancied he saw a small space between his dressing-gown and his football sweater – just enough for his Easter presents, he thought.

But Mr Wilkins thought otherwise. 'Certainly not, Jennings. I'm not putting any more in here – and that's flat,' he said, as he forced down the lid.

'It's not *quite* flat, sir: you'll have to stand on it,' Darbishire suggested helpfully. 'My father says there's an art in packing a trunk. You have to keep cool and calm, and use lots of patience. He says an ounce of patience is worth a ton of...'

'It's a pity your father isn't here! He'd be quite welcome to try his hand at this one,' said Mr Wilkins grimly.

'Yes, sir. And another thing my father says is– Oh, sir, you've left one of his legs hanging out!'

With a snort of exasperation, Mr Wilkins lifted the lid and tucked in the flapping pyjama trouser leg. At the same moment, Matron popped her head round the dormitory door to encourage the packer with a warm smile.

'Well, well! *Still* at it, Mr Wilkins?'

He assured her that he was!

'I'm sorry it's being so troublesome,' she went on. 'But all you've got to do is to remember to keep cool and calm, and use plenty of patience. I remember my mother used to say...'

Mr Wilkins leapt as though he had been

stung. 'Please, Matron, please! If anybody else starts telling me to keep cool and use patience, I'll ... I'll – well, I don't know *what* I'll do!'

When Matron had gone, Mr Wilkins closed the lid, sat on it, knelt on it and finally stood on it before the catches were securely in place.

'There, that's done the trick!' he panted. 'And what's more, Jennings, it can jolly well go without a rope round it, and chance its luck! Between you and me, I've had just about enough of your luggage, and I don't want to see it again for a long time.' He straightened his tie, put on his jacket and marched out of the room.

Jennings retrieved his Easter presents from underneath his bed. He stood toying with them absently, his gaze directed at the trunk in the middle of the floor. Finally he said: 'You know Darbi, there *was* a space between my dressing-gown and my football sweater – I saw it!'

Darbishire shrugged. 'Well, you've had it now! You won't get Old Wilkie to open it up again in a hurry.'

'No, I suppose not... But we could, couldn't we?'

'What?'

'Well, it isn't locked, and now it isn't even roped any more. We can slide the catches back without any trouble, and then the lid will open easily.'

'Maybe it will; but how are you going to close it again?'

Jennings scratched his nose thoughtfully with his clay pipe-rack. The trouble with Mr Wilkins' method, he maintained, was that it placed too much reliance on brute strength, and did not make use of the coolness, calmness and patience which Matron's mother and Darbishire's father recommended so strongly. Surely with more careful handling, it should be possible to squeeze his Easter presents into the little space he had noticed, and still close the lid with a carefree flourish!... What did Darbishire think?

'It *sounds* all right,' said Darbishire doubtfully. 'But I bet we'd come up against a few snags if we tried it.'

'Not if we do it scientifically. Where Old Wilkie goes wrong is that he belts into things like a bull on a bicycle, instead of planning out every move in advance. After all, your father said it ought to shut easily enough, and you believe what he says, don't you?'

'Oh, yes, of course! Still, I don't really think we ought...'

Darbishire was over-ruled: and a few seconds later the catches sprang from their sockets with loud clicks, as Jennings knelt down and eased them back with a pair of nail scissors.

A close inspection showed that there was less room to spare than he had thought. 'We'll have to squash everything down harder,' he said, as he buried his Easter gifts beneath his football sweater.

'But they won't *go* down any more!' Darbishire complained. 'You really want things like opera hats – they go down as flat as pancakes.'

'I don't think there's even room for a pancake. Besides, I'd look a bit feeble wearing an opera hat with school socks, wouldn't I?'

Darbishire bit his lip anxiously 'Gosh, it's going to be a tight squeeze. I've got a ghastly sort of feeling that we shan't be able to shut it... And *then*, what?'

Jennings rounded on him impatiently. 'Don't be such a mouldy pessimist, Darbishire! Your father wouldn't deliberately say it could be done, if he knew wizard well that it *couldn't!*'

'My father didn't say...'

'Oh, yes, he did: you just told me. So that proves it!'

'Ah, but what I meant was...' Darbishire tailed off: it seemed pointless to argue the matter. They would soon know, anyway!

The Easter presents were in by this time: Jennings rose to his feet, dusting his hand on the legs of his trousers.

All that remained to do was to close the lid

– and fasten it!

The dormitory bell was ringing as Mr
Carter walked along the corridor to the staff
room. He had dealt with most of the items
on his list, though he had yet to check
whether the end-of-term marks for Form 3
had been taken along to the headmaster's
study.

He found his colleague stretched out in
the only armchair that was not piled high
with text books and drawing-boards. Mr
Wilkins was relaxing; after coping so
strenuously in Dormitory 6, he felt in need
of a short rest to help him to regain his
strength.

'You look very comfortable, Wilkins! I only
wish *I* could find time to sit down and put
my feet up on the last night of term.'

'It was that wretched trunk, Carter. I'm
just about whacked! But I haven't forgotten
my marks, if that's what you've come about.
They're all ready. I'm going to take them
along as soon as I've got my breath back.'

A visit to the headmaster, to discuss some
last minute alterations in travelling arrangements was the next item on Mr Carter's list.
He offered to take the mark book with him.

'Thanks, Carter. It's on the table – a green
school exercise book with my initials on the
front, in pencil.'

There was no green exercise book on the

table when Mr Carter looked; but a quick glance showed one reposing on a pile of atlases some distance away. He picked it up and looked inside.

'This isn't the right one,' he said. 'It's full of scribble. Looks like some boy's private notebook.'

'That's got no business to be in here,' Mr Wilkins observed. 'I'm getting fed up with the way the staff room is used as a dumping ground for unwanted rubbish at the end of every term.'

'Yes, but the point is – where's your mark book? The Head's been waiting for it since before tea.'

With an effort, Mr Wilkins rose from his armchair. 'It's bound to be about somewhere. I'll have a look round.'

They searched for nearly twenty minutes – in cupboards and drawers, on the bookshelves, under the footballs in the corner. They sorted through the atlases and sifted the sheets of paper: there were so many places where a green exercise book might be concealed. But, after a thorough inspection of every likely and unlikely spot, they had to admit defeat.

'But this is ridiculous!' fumed Mr Wilkins, scavenging through the remains of old sheets of blotting paper in the bottom of the waste-paper basket. 'I *know* it's here. I distinctly remember leaving the book – well, somewhere in the room. I thought I put it on the table when I went downstairs for tea.'

Mr Carter shrugged his shoulders. 'Well, we've looked everywhere; and the only green-covered exercise book that isn't already tied up in a bundle is this one with the scribble in it.'

He opened the book once more – just to make sure he had made no mistake. He read: *February 10th – Got up. Got a letter from home. Got ticked off by Retsim Snikliw. Got a goal in football. Got two helpings of shepherd's pie. Went to bed... February 11th – Had piano lesson. Had football. Had to tidy the library. Had decent weather toddy.*

He laid down the book with a sigh. It seemed a poor reward for so much time spent in teaching Jennings to express his thoughts on paper.

'If only I'd taken it along to the study right away!' Mr Wilkins was saying. 'It was stopping to do that trunk that caused all the trouble.'

'I dare say, but that's neither here nor there at the moment. And unfortunately the same thing applies to your mark book,' Mr Carter observed. 'So there's only one thing to be done, Wilkins – you'll have to work the whole lot out again!'

'What!... But look here, I say, Carter – I couldn't possibly!... I'd have to stay up all night: those final positions in form have taken me hours to work out.'

'I should start right away, then. You've got about twelve hours before the train goes tomorrow morning.'

Mr Wilkins spread out his hands in a gesture of appeal. 'Yes, but dash it, Carter, it's – well, I mean, it's – dash it all, Carter!'

He made a quick mental review of the task involved. First, he would have to go round the school collecting up all the exercise books which had been used for his subjects during the term: he would have to work through them all, copying once again all the marks he had awarded to each boy since January 17th – nearly thirteen weeks ago! It meant adding up nearly ten thousand marks all over again. 'Ten thousand marks!' His lips moved silently as he repeated the formidable total to himself. Ten thousand marks – the task was fantastic ... incredible!

'I'll come and see how you're getting on, round about midnight, and bring you a cup of strong black coffee,' Mr Carter offered in tones of kindly sympathy. 'If you'd like to start straight away, I'll go and explain to the Head that you'll be working throughout the night, and that he can expect the final results by breakfast time tomorrow.'

'Yes, but – ten thousand marks! Just think of it!' Mr Wilkins sawed the air in wild gestures of frustration and despair. 'It's – it's maddening... It's – it's intolerable! How on earth am I going to...!'

There came a gentle knock on the staff room door. Mr Wilkins took no notice. 'I was hoping to get off in good time in the morning – and now *this* has to happen.'

Again, the knock on the door – louder this time.

'I feel so infuriated by the whole stupid business, I could – I could – well, I don't know *what* I could do!'

'You could see who's at the door,' Mr Carter suggested reasonably

'*Doh!*' Mr Wilkins rounded on his colleague with some heat. 'I've got something more important to do than to answer doors. Carter! I've got ten thousand marks to add up, and I'm in no mood to...'

This time there was no mistaking the urgency of the knock; Mr Wilkins swung round and glared at the door angrily

'Oh, come in – *come* in, if you must,' he cried at the top of his voice. 'Don't stand outside there, beating on the panels like a – like a panel beater!... Come *in!*'

Slowly the door opened a cautious six inches, and Jennings popped his head round. His mood was quiet and subdued, as though he felt uncertain of his welcome.

'Oh, it's you, is it, Jennings!... Well, get out!' said Mr Wilkins shortly

'Yes, sir... But, sir...!'

'Well, what is it, boy?'

Jennings gulped. 'Well, sir, please, sir; I hope I'm not disturbing you, but could you spare the time to come upstairs and fasten my trunk again, sir?'

16

Pack Up Your Troubles!

There is a time and place for everything. And this was certainly not the right moment to inform a harassed schoolmaster with ten thousand marks on his mind, that a hollow mockery had been made of his lid-lowering labours. And so it is not difficult to understand why there was a certain lack of warmth in the welcome extended to Jennings as he stood shuffling uncomfortably from one foot to the other on the threshold of the staff room.

Mr Carter *tut-tutted* in rebuke; while Mr Wilkins uttered a cry of anguish, clasped his hand to his brow and tottered blindly round in small circles.

Jennings waited for the master to cease revolving. Then he said: 'I'm terribly sorry, sir; but it was all Darbishire's father's fault. We used up an awful lot of patience – all we'd got, really – but it still won't shut, sir.'

'But what on earth did you want to *touch* the thing for, just after I'd got it shut, you silly little boy? I've never met such fatuous fat-headedness in my life! As though I hadn't got enough to do already without...!'

However, there was no point in wasting time in idle chat and curt comment. If the job had got to be done – then, the sooner the better! Muttering darkly Mr Wilkins strode out of the room and up the stairs to the dormitory.

Most of the boys were already in bed by this time, and the remainder were scuttling to and fro between bathroom and dormitory, wearing their overcoats or jackets in place of their dressing-gowns. There was a carefree, end-of-term feeling in the air, and Mr Wilkins was given a hearty reception when he arrived in Dormitory 6.

'Oh, hallo, sir; good evening, sir! Have you come to have another bash at Jennings' supersonic, jet-propelled, self-opening trunk lid, sir?' Bromwich major inquired in light-hearted tones.

'H'mph,' said Mr Wilkins.

'Isn't it wizard to think we're going home in a few hours from now, sir? Just think – no more work to do this term, sir!' twittered Atkinson.

'H'mph!' said Mr Wilkins.

'Are you feeling excited? I am, sir!' Temple confided. 'All sort of bottled-up with what-d'you-call-it, if you know what I mean, sir.'

'H'mph!' said Mr Wilkins.

'Have you worked out our maths marks yet, sir?... Where did I come in algebra, sir?'

asked Venables.

'Don't talk to me about marks!' said Mr Wilkins shortly. 'Or about feeling excited because there's no more work, either!' He made his way over to the trunk which had already wasted so much of his precious time. The lid was gaping open, the top layer of contents bulging over the side. Impatiently Mr Wilkins bundled them in; and had got as far as straining at the lid, when Matron came in to trace the owner of an unclaimed toothbrush.

'Good gracious – you're not *still* at it, Mr Wilkins?' she said, in surprise. 'Every time I come into this dormitory, I find you hard at work on the same trunk.'

'Urr-gurr-corwumph!' gasped the reluctant packer. 'It's no good, Matron; something will have to come out. We'll never do it with all this stuff inside.'

She looked at the bulging contents with a critical eye. 'Someone's been putting some more things in; it didn't look like this when I'd finished packing it.' She turned inquiringly to the owner of the trunk.

'Well, I only put my Easter presents in, Matron; and they were quite small, really. You see, I saw a little space, so...'

Mr Wilkins swivelled round rapidly. 'What's that? You mean to tell me you've been...! I – I– Corwumph! And I distinctly told you...!'

'Perhaps I'd better re-pack the top layer before you try again,' Matron suggested.

'There's nothing else for it; but let's not waste time. I've got a whole night's work ahead of me,' the master grumbled. With mounting impatience he seized the nearest garments and tossed them out; with them went the music books, which slithered on to the floor in an untidy litter of loose pages and torn covers.

Jennings knelt down and sorted the jumble of books into a neat stack. He took a furtive glance between the pages of *Silvery Waves*... Yes, his exercise book was still there, right enough: it wouldn't do to lose *that*, after all the trouble he had taken to...! He caught his breath in sudden astonishment as he noticed for the first time that the cover seemed slightly different from usual; it was cleaner – the ink stains had all disappeared!

Puzzled, he opened the book, and found that the pages which should have recorded the day-to-day events of the first fortnight of February, contained nothing more interesting than lists of names and meaningless rows of figures.

'Oh, fish-hooks; something's gone haywire!' he exclaimed. 'How did this get here?' He was overcome by a sudden feeling of dismay... His own book must still be in the staff room, if he had picked this one up by mistake... How stupid of him not to have made sure at the time! He would have seen then, that the book he now held in his hand was merely some used-up out-of-date volume fit for nothing but the waste-paper basket... A poor exchange, he reflected bitterly, for the interesting accounts he had written of the founding of the Form 3 museum.

He was recalled from his bitter reflections by the brusque tones of Mr Wilkins. 'What are you doing *now*, Jennings? If you've got that music tidied pass it over quickly – I'm in a hurry.'

'Yes, sir. I was just thinking about this old book I found. I thought it was my diary...'

'Good gracious, boy this is no time to start reading diaries!'

'I wasn't, sir. You see, this *isn't* my diary It's just some old scribble...'

'Well, it's not going in your trunk, what-ever it is.' Mr Wilkins seized the volume and prepared to toss it into the waste-paper basket.

But even as he took aim, he glanced down and noticed that the book had a green cover – that the initials L P W were pencilled on the front – and that inside were ten thousand marks, neatly totalled in his own handwriting.

'Good heavens – my mark book!' he cried, in ringing tones. 'Well, I... Bless my... How on earth... Good heavens!'

After the first joyful rapture of discovery, he turned again to the pyjama-clad figure kneeling beside him on the floor. 'Did *you* put this book in here, Jennings?'

The boy swallowed hard. 'I must have done, sir; but I didn't mean to. I meant to put mine in, because it was only thin. I'm awfully sorry sir. It was just a sort of accidental bish – er – a mistake, I should say.' Diffidently he added: 'I suppose you've still got my book in the staff room then, sir?'

'I believe I did see some horrible scribble – yes,' snorted Mr Wilkins.

'Oh, I'm so glad it's safe, sir. It's rather an important book, you see,' Jennings confided. 'And is *your* book important too, sir?'

Mr Wilkins made a noise like an exploding vacuum-flask.

'Is it important?' he echoed, waving the volume in the air like a linesman's flag. *'Is it important?* We've searched the staff room high and low for this book, you silly little boy! It's got ten thousand marks in it – *ten thousand marks!'*

The memory of his anguish returned, and he rose to his feet with a determined expression in his eye. 'You've caused an endless amount of trouble by your stupidity Jennings, and you deserve to be very soundly punished... You'll come along with me to the headmaster's study immediately.'

'Yes, sir,' Jennings mumbled unhappily.

Matron had been following the little drama with interest; and now that it threatened to end on a note of tragedy she decided to intervene.

'Oh, but, Mr Wilkins – this is the last night of term!' she pointed out.

'I daresay it is, Matron but this is a very serious business, and the boy deserves to be dealt with in no uncertain manner. He waved a large forefinger in her direction to underline the importance of the matter. 'Why, do you realise, Matron, that if I hadn't got this book back, I should have had to stay up all night, doing my marks over again. *All night*, Matron – think of it!'

Matron thought of it. And then, with simple feminine reasoning, she said: 'But you *have* got it back, Mr Wilkins! You ought to be feeling ever so pleased, now.' She waved a slim forefinger in his direction to emphasise the logic of her argument. 'Why, don't you realise, Mr Wilkins, that Jennings has just saved you from the ordeal of staying up all night!'

Mr Wilkins opened his eyes in surprise. It was a way of looking at it that had not occurred to him. For some moments he stood pondering the matter: her argument was, of course, a very flimsy one, he told himself – just the sort of thing a woman *would* suggest!... All the same, it was the last evening of term ... and he *had* got his mark book back ... and he certainly *did* feel pleased about it...!

Beneath his blustery manner, Mr Wilkins had a kind heart and sometimes – very seldom, but *sometimes* – it swayed him against his better judgement. It did so, then.

'H'mph... M'yes. I – er – well, perhaps this wouldn't be a very good moment to go and see the headmaster,' he muttered gruffly. 'He's bound to be busy considering it's the last night of term.'

'Oh, thank you, sir!' said Jennings.

'Don't thank me, boy – thank Matron,' barked Mr Wilkins. And then, unexpectedly, the angry look faded, and his vast, booming laugh rang round the dormitory as he turned to Matron and said: 'I think I'll put my book in my pocket, out of harm's way before anyone else starts packing it. It's a weight off my mind to have it back, I don't mind telling you.'

'It's a weight off my mind, too, sir,' said Jennings. 'I'd have had a supersonic shock when I got home and found I'd only got Form Three's maths marks to copy into my diary.'

'Speaking of weight, would you like to kneel on the lid again, Mr Wilkins,' Matron asked, as she put the last of the articles into the trunk. By skilful arrangement, she had managed to include not only the music, but also the Easter presents as well.

'Right you are, Matron! No point in being fourteen stone if you can't put it to good use, eh?' said Mr Wilkins. Once more he bent his back to the task. 'Urr-wurr-gurrwumph!' he panted, as the last catch snapped into position with a loud click.

The last breakfast of term is always a little different from the other meals which have gone before. In the dining-hall the atmosphere is livelier, the conversation louder than usual. Appetites lose their mid-term keenness, for no one can devote himself seriously to porridge and hard-boiled egg, when his thoughts are spiced with the excitement of returning home after three months' absence.

'I'm not going to eat my egg now: I'm going to put it in my pocket and have it on the train,' Venables announced. 'I've got at least an hour's journey and I don't want to collapse from starvation before I get home.'

Bromwich major pushed his porridge away untasted, took a piece of bread and reached for the cruet. He mixed himself an unsavoury sandwich-filling of pepper, salt and mustard which he stirred well with his teaspoon; then he spread the mixture thickly on his bread and took a large bite.

'Ugh! Ghastly muck! Fancy expecting us to eat stuff like that,' he complained, grimacing at the unappetising flavour. 'That's jolly well the last mouthful of mouldy school food I'm going to eat for a whole month!'

It was, perhaps, an unfair test of the Linbury Court catering arrangements; but he felt that he would enjoy his meals at home much more, if he could compare them with this last distasteful memory of school food.

Mr Carter went round the tables to see that no one had yet lost the railway ticket he had been given on the previous evening. Nobody had – though Blotwell spent an anxious ten minutes emptying his pockets and sorting through two dozen cheese labels, a packet of foreign stamps and a collection of match-box tops, before finding the missing ticket tucked in the top of his sock, where he had placed it for safety.

After breakfast, the boys gathered outside on the quad to wait for the special school bus to take them to the station. And as they waited, they sang:

'This time tomorrow, where shall I be?
    Miles away from Lin-bur-y.
No more spiders in my tea,
    No more sleeping in a dormit'ry.'

This, too, was a gross slander on Matron's hygienic standards of housekeeping; but she didn't seem to mind! Both she and Mr Wilkins were outside amongst the crowd – engulfed in a wave of farewells.

'Goodbye, Matron, in case I don't see you again before the bus comes... Goodbye, sir! See you next term, sir!'

'Goodbye, Venables; goodbye, Temple and Atkinson!' Matron had to shout to make herself heard above the hubbub.

Mr Wilkins didn't need to shout. His normal breezy tone drowned all other voices as he boomed: 'Goodbye, Darbishire – have a good holiday... Goodbye, Jennings – don't practice the piano too hard – it wouldn't do to have a nervous breakdown before next term, eh! Ha-ha-ha!'

Jennings and Darbishire gathered together the last-minute odds and ends for which they could find no room in their suitcases. Darbishire's hairbrush and face flannel would have to travel home in his trouser pocket: the brown paper parcel which Jennings clutched so carefully contained his assortment of salvage and – more important – the green exercise book which he had been allowed to retrieve from the staff room.

'I'm jolly glad Old Wilkie let me have it back,' he confided to Darbishire. 'He's jolly decent, really – or rather, he doesn't seem *quite* so mouldy, when you know you're not going to see him again till next term.'

There were still a few minutes before the bus was due when Mr Carter came out on to the quad to see them off.

'Aren't you coming with us, sir?' Jennings asked.

'No, not this time. The headmaster's taking the London train.'

'Goodbye then, sir. I hope you have a supersonic holiday sir.'

'Thank you, Jennings. Are you quite sure you've got everything packed at last?'

The boy grinned. 'Oh, yes, sir – even my famous diary. I've got to keep it up for Aunt Angela's sake. Still, there's only another two hundred and seventy-five days to go now, so I reckon that ten shillings she mentioned is as good as mine already.' He produced the small red book and the larger green one from the depths of his brown paper bag, and passed them over for the master's inspection. 'There, sir! I told you at the beginning of the term that I wasn't going to miss a day; and I haven't, sir – you see!'

'Well, you've certainly had plenty to write about this term, what with alleged Roman remains and missing mark books,' Mr Carter replied, with a smile. 'And I seem to remember hearing a most amazing rumour connecting your diary with incredulous policemen and European spy rings – but perhaps I'm not supposed to know about that!'

He skimmed through the books, pausing here and there to read an entry... *Weather fairly decent toddy. Won a vase with a gun for Nortam but gave her flowers... Dug a relic up with fork and Erihsibrad; had liquorice allsorts... Saw a policeman this day, but in bedroom slippers as he was indoors... Went to Mus. on bus... Helped Mr W pack my trunk. Weather fairly decent toddy...*

Mr Carter handed back the books. They seemed to him to provide a somewhat sketchy understatement of the more hair-raising events of the term. 'H'm; well, all I can say is, Jennings, that if your generous Aunt Angela is willing to part with ten shillings for such a meagre record as that, whatever would she pay if she knew the whole story?'

The bus arrived then, and the chattering crowd swarmed aboard and took their seats. The headmaster followed; and in less than a minute the seventy-nine boarders of Linbury Court School were speeding down the drive on their way to the station.

Mr Carter watched till the bus rounded the bend of the drive. Then he went back to his study. 'Weather fairly decent toddy!' he murmured sadly to himself, as he climbed the stairs. 'A year's work in English composition – and what does it amount to?... *Fairly decent toddy!'*

This Large Print Book, for people
who cannot read normal print,
is published under the auspices of

THE ULVERSCROFT FOUNDATION

... we hope you have enjoyed this book.
Please think for a moment about those
who have worse eyesight than you ...
and are unable to even read or enjoy
Large Print without great difficulty.

You can help them by sending a
donation, large or small, to:

**The Ulverscroft Foundation,
1, The Green, Bradgate Road,
Anstey, Leicestershire, LE7 7FU,
England.**
or request a copy of our brochure for
more details.

The Foundation will use all donations
to assist those people who are visually
impaired and need special attention
with medical research, diagnosis
and treatment.

Thank you very much for your help.